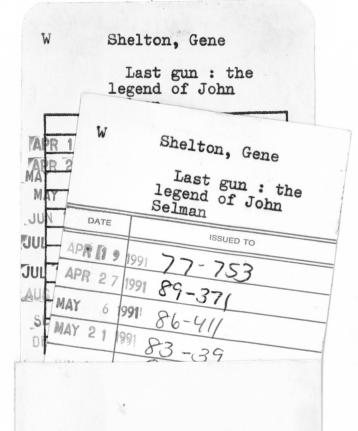

W   Shelton, Gene

           Last gun : the
           legend of John

W   Shelton, Gene

           Last gun : the
           legend of John
           Selman

DATE	ISSUED TO
APR 1 9 1991	77-753
APR 2 7 1991	89-371
MAY 6 1991	86-411
MAY 2 1 1991	83-39

APR 1
APR 2
MA
MAY
JUN
JUL
JUL
AUG
SE
DE

TEXAS LEGENDS ★ BOOK 1

LAST GUN"

The Legend
of John Selman

GENE SHELTON

A DOUBLE D WESTERN
DOUBLEDAY
New York London Toronto Sydney Auckland

A DOUBLE D WESTERN
PUBLISHED BY DOUBLEDAY
a division of Bantam Doubleday Dell Publishing Group, Inc.
666 Fifth Avenue, New York, New York 10103

A DOUBLE D WESTERN, DOUBLEDAY,
and the portrayal of the letters DD
are trademarks of Doubleday, a division of
Bantam Doubleday Dell Publishing Group, Inc.

Library of Congress-Cataloging-in-Publication Data

Shelton, Gene.
Last gun: the legend of John Selman/by Gene Shelton. — 1st ed.
  p. cm. — (Texas legends: bk. 1) (A Double D western)
  1. Selman, John Henry, 1839–1896—Fiction. 2. Texas—History—
1846–1950—Fiction. I. Title. II. Series.
PS3569.H39364L3 1991
813'.54—dc20 90-43172
CIP

ISBN 0-385-41410-2
Copyright © 1991 by Gene Shelton
All Rights Reserved
Printed in the United States of America
March 1991
First Edition

10 9 8 7 6 5 4 3 2 1

To Theresa—
  Whose faith and confidence in her father kept me going when my own faltered, this work is dedicated with love.

FOREWORD

This is a work of fiction based on the life of John Henry Selman, one of the Old West's deadliest and yet least-known gunfighters.

Some of the characters appearing in this book actually existed, but no conclusions should be drawn as to their real-life personalities, motivations, or actions on the basis of this story.

Many of the characters and events herein are purely the creation of the author.

Every effort has been made to portray as accurately as possible the actual dates, locations, and sequence of events that shaped the life of John Selman.

ACKNOWLEDGMENTS

The author wishes to express his appreciation to the many librarians, fellow Western writers, and historians whose assistance made this book possible.

A special tip of the hat is offered to Leon C. Metz of El Paso, Texas, the eminent historian on gunfighters of the Old West and author of many authoritative biographies of the famous and infamous figures of the West. It was Leon's biographical study, *John Selman, Gunfighter*, that became the author's accepted "bible" in resolving the frequently conflicting accounts of Selman's life and times.

Profuse thanks also to Janice A. Reese of the Moody Texas Ranger Library in Waco, Texas, who was never more than a phone call or a mailbox away when a specific question arose in the preparation of this manuscript.

GENE SHELTON
Sulphur Springs, Texas

LAST GUN

ONE

Arroyo Blanco
North Texas, Spring 1863

The rifleman knelt at the shallow notch in the rocky creek-bed, muzzle of the fifty-two Sharps rifle trained on the grove of post oak trees four hundred yards away. He saw no movement, but he knew the four Comanches were still there.

He glanced toward the bright sky. Buzzards wheeled above the crumpled figures, one thirty yards from the arroyo, another a hundred paces further back. There had been six of them to begin with.

"Come on, damn you," he muttered toward the trees. His words slurred around the linen cartridge clamped between his teeth. "Let's get it over with."

The rifleman knew the Comanches wouldn't make the same mistakes again. The raiders' good medicine at finding a white man riding alone had gone sour. It had cost them two of their braves. Now they would respect the lone rider and the way he handled a long gun.

More than the white man's scalp and revenge for their dead, he knew, the Indians wanted his horse and his weapon. A Sharps was a prized commodity on the Texas frontier. They also wanted their dead. The last thing a Comanche would leave behind was a fallen comrade. Behind him in the bottom of the narrow ravine, the bay snorted and stomped, nostrils flared, his instinct to run held in check by months of training. *Good horse,* the man thought; *too good to be ruined by a damn Comanche. Worse comes to worst, I'll shoot the bay; no Indian's going to ride John Selman's horse.*

John pulled the heavy Army Colt forty-four pistol from his belt holster. He checked the loads and caps and placed the handgun alongside the rifle within easy reach.

He heard the yelps of the Comanches before they charged from the shelter of the trees. Two rode straight toward him, quirting their horses into a dead run; two others veered away, one north, one south. It was obvious they intended to flank the man in the arroyo.

John thumbed the Sharps to full cock and centered the sights on the chest of one Comanche, ignoring the other three. *One at a time, Selman,* he cautioned himself. *You can't afford to get careless now.* The Indian grew larger in his sights. Two hundred yards. One-fifty. A hundred.

John squeezed the trigger. The stock of the Sharps slammed against his shoulder. Through the thunder of muzzle blast and blue-gray smoke, he heard the solid whop of the heavy slug against flesh. The Indian tumbled over the rump of his horse. The second Comanche abruptly wheeled his horse to John's right and disappeared into a grove of cottonwoods sixty yards down-creek.

John broke the action of the Sharps, plucked the linen cartridge from between his teeth, rammed it into the breech, and snapped the action closed. He felt the slight rip as the knife edge on the block snipped the trailing edge of the linen from the cartridge. He swung the barrel toward the trees where the second Comanche had disappeared.

He saw nothing, and heard nothing but the slight ringing in his ears from the muzzle blast of the Sharps. Sweat trickled down his back and from beneath his hatband. He felt the steady thump of his heart against his ribs as he waited. The rolling echoes of the rifle shot died away, leaving the silence of the short-grass prairie broken only by the sigh of a light breeze. John thought he could almost hear the tick of his pocket watch.

He winced as a rifle ball slammed into the creek bank inches from his head, and dirt and gravel laced into his cheek. Smoke billowed from a wild plum thicket along the arroyo forty yards downstream. John slapped a shot toward the center of the smoke and heard a startled grunt of surprise and pain. Maybe a hit, maybe not. He picked up the handgun, sent a ball after the rifle shot. A Comanche half stood, then staggered forward. John shot again. The Indian fell.

John put down the revolver and reloaded the Sharps, his movements quick and mechanical, without need for thought.

Beyond the fallen Indian a blue jay squawked in indignation and fluttered from the branches of a dead tree. John held the sights of the rifle on the bleached trunk. The call of a bobwhite quail sounded from the north and was answered from the south. They had him bracketed. The calls had been from close by. John wiped a moist palm against his shirt. *If it ends here, at least, by God, they'll know they've been in a scrap.*

A rifle barrel appeared at the side of the dead tree, part of a dark face showing behind it. John fired by instinct, heard the thump of the slug against wood, and knew his shot had gone wild. He ducked as smoke billowed from the Comanche's musket, then felt the air rustle as the ball went overhead. He heard the click of a stone behind him and grabbed for the Colt as he spun toward the sound. A half-dozen paces away a Comanche stood, rifle muzzle swinging toward John's chest. John yanked the pistol into line and squeezed the trigger. The hammer of the handgun fell with the empty metallic click of a misfire. He braced himself for the bullet shock as he thumbed the hammer of the Colt. He knew he would be too late. Then the Indian's head snapped to the side and the rifle spun away. The heavy blast of a big-bore weapon hammered John's ears. The Comanche pitched forward, moccasins digging at the creek sand in death throes.

John stared at the Indian's body, momentarily confused. Then the pound of horse's hooves down-creek jolted him back to reality. He caught a glimpse of the last Comanche, leaning low on his pony's neck and quirting the animal hard. John fired twice at the fleeing Indian, but knew as he pulled the trigger that the range was too great for the handgun.

John thrust the pistol into his waistband and reloaded the Sharps. Somebody was still out there. Apparently a friend, but John was in no hurry to make a move. Or a mistake.

"Hey, white man!" The call was clear and strong in the still springtime air. "You still wearing some hair?"

The words were in English, and the accent was familiar.

John heaved a sigh of relief. "Plenty hair left," he called in the Tonkawa language. "You in the market for it?"

"Not today. Huntin' Comanch. Could use a chew, though, you got a spare plug. Didn't know you spoke the tongue."

A stocky Indian slouched into view, long-barrelled percussion rifle held at the ready. Fresh sweat streaked his once-blue shirt, working its way through days of accumulated grime. The Tonkawa nodded a casual greeting, then strode past John to the downed Comanche in the plum thicket. John watched without expression as the Tonkawa raised his rifle and fired.

"That one was still alive. Good Comanch now." The Tonkawa reloaded as he walked back to John, then squatted on his heels, rifle in the crook of an arm, and deftly caught the plug of tobacco John tossed to him.

"You got a name, white man?"

"Selman. John Selman."

The Tonkawa slipped a heavy-bladed knife from his belt, sliced off a portion of the tough tobacco quid, and slipped it into his mouth. "My name's Pete, John Selman. Christened King James Peter Wolfpelt. My mother had a severe attack of Christianity just before I was born. She got over it. Most white men call me Whiskey Pete." He tossed the tobacco plug back to John.

"It appears," John said, "that I'm in your debt. That Comanche had me dead in his sights."

King James Peter Wolfpelt shrugged. "No bother." He chewed for a moment in silence, then spat an amber stream into the sand. "Could say you did most of my work for me. Damn Comanch. Been trackin' that bunch six days now. Renegades. Wild bucks from old Red Hand's clan. Raided my cousin's place, killed him and his wife, took four good horses." He rolled the chew in his mouth. "I stole the horses back three nights out. Hell, there ain't no Comanch can hold a candle to a Tonk when it comes to stealin' horses. Or anything else. You want the scalps?"

John shook his head. "Not this time. You take them." John Selman had no use for scalps, but he knew they were important to the Tonk. To him they meant his relatives who died at Comanche hands could find peace in the afterlife, and the dead Comanche would walk the darkness, never to be born again until all their body parts were buried.

Pete nodded. "Obliged. I'll be back shortly. Appreciate it if you didn't punch a hole in me with that damn buffalo gun. Could ruin a man's outlook on life."

While the Tonkawa went about his business John reloaded the Colt. *Hell of a time for a misfire,* he thought as he examined the primer cap that had failed to ignite. *My scalp would be on that Comanche's belt by now if the Tonk hadn't been around.*

He stripped the saddle from the bay to let the horse's back cool and the blanket dry. He lifted another half-dozen linen Sharps cartridges from a saddle pouch, dropped them in a shirt pocket, then cocked the rifle and checked the priming magazine. The self-primer mechanism was a small but valuable improvement in the Sharps. It saved a couple of seconds per shot. The rifle had cost him a month's army pay and the winnings from two poker games, but it was worth the price. Hit something with a Sharps and it stayed hit.

John listened to Whiskey Pete whistle a tune from the Methodist hymnal as he lifted the Comanche scalps.

Pete was back in little more than a quarter hour. The buzzards already were lumbering in to tear at the bodies in the short grass.

"Well, Pete, what do we do about the one who got away?"

Pete shrugged. "Let him go. Be much wailing in old Red Hand's camp when that one gets back. Hard for that Comanch to say how come six braves couldn't handle one white man and one Tonk. If he don't do the smart thing and lie about it." Pete wiped the stained knife blade on his trouser leg, leaving a streak of gore on the cloth. "Where you headed, John Selman?"

"Sherman, over in Grayson County." John pulled his army canteen from a saddle pouch and handed it to the Tonk. Pete glanced at the CSA stamp on the container, raised an eyebrow, then lifted the canteen and drank. "You army?"

"Up until a few days ago. Fort Washita."

Pete twisted the cap back onto the canteen and handed it to John. "Now it ain't none of this Injun's business," the Tonkawa said, "but you seem to be a tad lost for somebody headed from Washita to Sherman. Best I remember, Sherman's quite a ways east of this place."

"I sort of decided to stay off the main roads," John said. "The army didn't plan on me leaving so soon. I signed up to fight

Yankees and they sent me to a place where there wasn't anything to do but make sure some Choctaw didn't stray off the reservation. Choctaws there got no intention of going anywhere. I got bored with the whole setup."

Pete grunted in understanding. "Nothin' wasted worse than a warrior whose chiefs don't know how to use him." He stared at John for a moment, then extended a hand. His grip was firm, the palm and fingers calloused. "Best be on my way. Got one of the ugliest and crankiest squaws the Creator ever made waitin' for me back home. John Selman, you one hell of a Comanche fighter. Maybe we meet again some day."

"I hope so, Pete. And thanks again."

"None needed." The Tonkawa mounted and nodded toward John's big bay. "That's a good horse. If I wasn't civilized and you didn't have that big rifle, and you had the common decency to let them Comanch get a slug into you, I'd be tempted to take him myself."

The Tonkawa kneed his horse about. John Selman watched until the Indian vanished from view over the west side of the arroyo. He listened to the raucous hiss of the feeding buzzards, then saddled the bay. It was still a long ride to Sherman. Back to the family and the girl he had left eighteen months ago. And the uncertain future that lay beyond the reunion.

Sherman, Texas
Spring 1863

Edna deGraffenreid sat primly on the porch swing of her frame home and swallowed against the ache in her throat. She silently vowed not to let John Selman see any tears.

"I'm not much good at saying goodbye, Edna. Especially so soon." John leaned against the porch railing a respectful distance from the dark-haired young woman. "But I'm not going back to the army and this is the first place they would look for me. I've a widowed mother and younger brothers and sisters to care for. And I don't have a thing to offer you. Not now."

"I understand, John." Edna tried to control the tremor in her voice. "I know you've got no choice." She squared her shoulders. "Jasper will be glad to see you."

"Your brother's a good man. And there's plenty of ways a man can make something of himself out in the Brazos country. I'll come back for you, Edna. If you're still interested by then."

Edna fought back the urge to go to John Selman and embrace him. But that wouldn't be proper. She was sixteen now, and must conduct herself like a lady. She also knew that her mother was probably watching through the lace curtains of the window at her back. That was enough to keep a girl's conduct proper. "I'll be here, John."

Edna thought she saw a flicker of relief, and at the same time sadness, in the pale blue eyes of the man at the porch rail.

"I couldn't ask for more, Edna." John placed his hat on his head, touched the brim, then turned and walked away.

Edna watched him go, easy strides carrying his muscular five-foot-ten frame away from her once more. "God ride with you, John," she whispered, "and bring you back safely to me."

Clear Fork of the Brazos
Texas Frontier, Summer 1863

John Selman re-coiled the Plymouth manila hemp rope as he watched the wild-eyed Longhorn cow charge into the edge of the thicket in scorched indignation.

She had been one of the "slicks"—cattle unbranded and free for the taking—but now she wore the Selman Four Clubs brand, along with a couple dozen others like her. John had grown to enjoy the acrid odor of burned hide and hair. It smelled of a beginning, of money. Of respectability and a future free of want.

He loosened the double-rigged saddle cinches to let the lathered bay blow for a few minutes, catching its wind while the branding ring cooled. Horse and man both wore the signs of the chase. The bay's sweat-slicked sides and deep chest sported some fresh scrapes and beads of blood from a pair of small cuts. A sleeve of John's shirt hung by two fingers of cloth. A shallow scratch smarted over his bearded cheek, and his palm stung from a rope burn when he had been a little slow with the dally, the double wrap of the rope around the horn of his heavy Mexican saddle.

He was satisfied. The cow had been worth the chase; she was young and strong. She would do her part to build the Selman herd in the years to come.

John Selman knew he had found a home.

This, he reflected, was a man's country. Water was plentiful in the river and spring-fed creeks of the numerous shallow arroyos and deeper canyons. Groves of trees and rocky outcrops provided shelter for the cattle when winter winds screeched down from Indian Territory just across the Red River to the north. Buffalo were thick on the open plains a few hours' ride to the west. The breaks along the Brazos teemed with deer and small game. A man could feed his family well from the land while building a herd.

The hills here and to the south held hundreds of wild cattle like the one he had just claimed. In a way, it was like the farm of his youth in the Arkansas hills, but better. Here, the bulls did the planting, the cows produced the crop, and all a man need do was see to the harvest.

The work was bone-deep, dangerous, and lasted from first light until sundown. It was also, John told himself with a smile, a lot more fun than any store clerk would ever have.

John no longer had to look over his shoulder for Confederate troops in search of a deserter. The undermanned garrison at Camp Cooper a few miles to the south dwindled by the day. The few remaining troops would be pulling out within the month. Even before the pullout was planned, the soldiers had shown no interest in John. Maybe they didn't know he was a deserter. Or just didn't care. It was all the same to John Selman.

The only blotch on the tranquility of the Clear Fork was Indians. The settlers were deep into Kiowa and Comanche country. The Comanche in particular were growing bolder by the day as army troops pulled back from the Texas frontier. There was no doubt in John's mind that when the final troops left Camp Cooper, the civilians along the Clear Fork would be up to their butts in Indian war parties.

John stroked the bay's neck to let the gelding knew it had done its job well. He breathed in the smell of horse sweat and wondered how some people could find it offensive. The scent of a horse was rich to the nostrils, complemented by the distinct smell of oiled leather. To John Selman, the blend of odors in the clearing was as soothing as anything he had ever experienced.

He retrieved the now-cool branding ring from beside the ashes of the small fire, tied it to the saddle, and glanced toward the western sun. It was too late in the day to start the hunt for another slick. They would still be there tomorrow.

"John!"

The call came from a ridge above the brush thicket. John's hand slapped the stock of the Sharps. The weapon was partway from the saddle boot before recognition checked John's instincts.

"Down here, Tom!" he called.

Tom Selman rode into the clearing moments later, his slender but strong body seemingly dwarfed by the big roan horse under him. Tom was fourteen now, nine years younger than John, but old enough to know how to use the Springfield forty-five-seventy carbine in the crook of his arm and the Navy thirty-six revolver tucked into his waistband.

"Ma wants you."

John bit back an impulse to give the youngster a tongue-lashing for going out alone in a country where there could be an Indian behind every rock. He knew their mother wouldn't have sent Tom unless it was urgent. He pulled the cinches tight and swung into the saddle. When the Widow Selman summoned, her offspring answered.

Mrs. Jeremiah Selman sat at the head of the table, her lips set in a thin line as she stirred milk into the teacup before her. Tea seemed to be the Widow Selman's only indulgence.

John sat patiently at her right, Tom at her left. Sisters Mary Ann, Lucinda, and Elizabeth had suspended the usual girl-talk, quarrels, and giggles, and went quietly about their household chores. The Widow Selman would speak when she was ready and not before.

John admitted that even he was somewhat in awe of the Widow Selman when there was serious business afoot. There was a quiet, solid strength in the slender, stooped body that even strangers seemed to recognize. Within days of the Selman family's arrival on the Clear Fork, she had become the one sought out when a neighbor fell ill or was injured, or a baby needed to be brought into the world. She could be as gentle as a spring wind or as tough as a blacksmith's anvil. *Without women like her,* John thought, *there wouldn't be a Texas. Or a need for one.*

The Widow Selman clinked her spoon into the saucer. "John, you've done a fine job of providing for this family. With Tom's help, of course. We've never wanted for food or shelter, and I respect all the hard work you've put into building the herd—for us and for Edna. Now, I've something to ask of you."

The Widow Selman paused for a sip of tea, and gazed over the rim of the cup at John. "Other people along the river need you, son. With the army leaving, there won't be a thing to hold the Indians in check. Just this morning, a rider came by. Kiowas raided the Jacobs farm and took all their stock yesterday afternoon."

"Anyone hurt?"

"No. Jacobs and his boy fought them off, but the family's ruined. Those poor people . . ." Her voice trailed away in sympathy. She sighed. "Anyway, there's a meeting tomorrow night at Press McCarty's ranch. He's asked every settler within thirty miles to come. Something has to be done about the Indians. There's talk of forming our own company of state militia. Without a good leader, the volunteer troops would be little more than a joke. John, you've got the qualities. I've talked to some of the other women and a few of the men. Your name will be put in nomination as lieutenant for the company."

John started to object. "But there are other men—"

"None like you, John Selman," his mother interrupted. There seemed to be a gleam of pride in her eyes. "Besides, John, consider this—if you are an officer of a company of Texas State Troops, the Confederacy should be more prone to overlook your, shall we say, transgression."

John fell silent for a moment, considering his mother's arguments. There was merit to them. But it would take time away from his effort to build the Four Clubs herd. Time away from the day when he would go to Sherman for Edna.

"The people of the Clear Fork need you, John. *We* need you. I want the best man for the job protecting my family."

John sighed in resignation. "I'll take it on, if the others want me."

"Good, son. You always were a sensible man."

"What about me?" Tom's words held a quarrelsome edge.

The Widow Selman shook her head. "I'd like you to stay with the family, Tom. We'll need a man here to protect us while John is off chasing Indians or bandits."

Tom's features twisted in a grimace. John stared at his younger brother for a moment. He had never been able to understand Tom, to get inside his head. The boy was moody and withdrawn. He seldom spoke, but when he did there was a bitterness in his tone that belied his years. John sensed a quiet violence within Tom, a tension just below the surface like a fiddle string stretched to its limit. But he was a good hand with a gun and a competent tracker.

"Tom could ride with us when he isn't needed here, Mother," John said. "He's a grown man now." It was as close to defiance of the Widow Selman as John cared to get. Her nod of agreement took him by surprise.

"If you're going to be a leader, John Selman, you have the right to pick your men," she said.

John Selman lounged against a wall of the crowded main room of Press McCarty's ranch house. Tobacco smoke painted swirling blue patterns around the tallow lamps. Several whiskey bottles sat unopened on the table in the center of the room.

The assembled crowd included most of the ranchers and farmers with claims along the Clear Fork, businessmen with various outposts along the river, teamsters, hunters, cowboys, and a number of strangers. On the whole, John concluded, a gathering of tough men. All were armed, some with ancient flintlock shotguns, a few with modern rifles and handguns.

The formation of the Stephens County Company of the Texas Home Guard had taken less than a quarter-hour. John Selman was elected lieutenant by a vote of sixteen to two.

John glanced at the only other nominee. Slim Gentry, a bandy-legged man known for his nasty disposition and a mean streak, glared at the new lieutenant in open contempt. *I'm going to have trouble with that possum-faced little bastard sooner or later,* John thought as he turned away from Gentry, ignoring the man's stare.

Press McCarty tapped a knife blade against a water glass to call for quiet, and waited for the mutter of the crowd to fade. "Gentlemen," McCarty said, "it's time now to get on with other plans. Maybe the Camp Cooper troops wasn't much help to begin with, but they kept the Indians more or less honest. Now, the damn savages are comin' right to our back door, and they ain't askin' for biscuits and honey. They're huntin' scalps and horses."

"Press is right," said one lanky rancher seated at the table. "Not a man of us doesn't go to bed at night worried. Most of us have lost horses, mules, or beeves. A few of us have lost people, too."

McCarty jabbed the knife point into the tabletop. "If we're goin' to be safe in our own homes, it's up to us." He nodded toward John. "Selman's militia company's a start, but it ain't enough. I say it's time we fort up. Get as many of our people as we can in one spot. Scattered out like we are now, it's the same as invitin' a Comanche to come right on in and help himself."

McCarty paused for a few heartbeats. "Gents," he said, "I don't know about you, but I ain't gonna stand by and see no women's hair on lodgepoles. No more kids carried off and made over into savages."

A tall, spare man in a wrinkled linen suit stood. "Mister McCarty, I've something to say, if you don't mind."

Press McCarty nodded in the man's direction. "Most of you folks here know Sam Newcomb. Sam, speak your piece."

"I have claim to several parcels of land on the north side of the Clear Fork," Newcomb said. "There are several families living near there now. It's on open ground with a spring and well water and can easily be defended from attack. I will offer to those of you who have families choice building spots on that land."

"What'll it cost us, Newcomb?" The question from a farmer was tinged with suspicion.

"Not a cent," Newcomb said. "All I want is to see the place named after a great man—Jefferson Davis—and I want you all to agree that a schoolhouse be built."

Press McCarty twisted the cork from a bottle, dribbled a double shot into a water glass, and raised the whiskey.

"To Fort Davis, gentlemen," he said.

Fort Davis
Spring 1865

John Selman lashed the final sapling into place on the roof of the new house in Fort Davis, and paused to survey his surroundings. Below, in what was soon to be the Selman family's front yard, Tom leaned against the wagon and sipped at a dipper of water from the nearby well.

The community of Fort Davis was not a fort in the normal sense of the word. John sensed it never would be. Still, one did not argue with the Widow Selman. When she declared that she hadn't borne a family to supply scalps for some heathen Indians, the issue was settled. The Selmans would become residents of Fort Davis.

Despite his ties to the downriver site where the growing Four Clubs herd grazed, John had not protested. His mother had been right. The young settlement just to the north of the Clear Fork of the Brazos offered considerably better protection than did the original Selman ranch house some seven miles away.

The small cluster of Fort Davis homes housed maybe a hundred and twenty residents, mostly adults with a few young people and a sprinkling of children. John calculated at least eighty guns could be brought into play if needed—many of them in the hands of women like the Widow Selman, who could thump a Bible or thumb a hammer just as well as some of the men.

Sam Newcomb's schoolhouse was already in operation. John had chosen a lot next to it for the new Selman home. The schoolhouse had gone up first, followed by a simple one-room church. It had no steeple; the small whitewashed wooden cross outside was sufficient. The third new building, Turk Bartlett's place, was a double structure, half residence and half saloon. The women of Fort Davis, including the Widow Selman, weren't overly fond of that, but they knew compromises were necessary in dangerous times.

Most of the homes, like John's, were made of pickets. The lack of suitable building materials and the expense of hauling lumber from as far away as Fort Worth meant the builders had to make do with what was available. John and Tom had spent most of two days selecting, cutting, and hauling small trees and saplings to the site from the hills and river breaks. Another day and the pickets were in place. All that remained now was the cutting of prairie sod chunks to cover the roof, and then the tedious chore of mixing native grass and mud to chink the holes and gaps in the walls.

The fort had been born in a frenzy of work, optimism, and the frequently voiced fear of Indian raids and outlaw Jayhawkers thundering down from the north to pillage the community. More than a few of the residents seemed more afraid of the Jayhawkers than the Indians, John thought. Two blockhouses were partially finished, and leaders of the settlement planned for the day when the entire village would be surrounded by a fortlike stockade.

The men who gathered at Fort Davis were a mixed lot. Most were family men hoping to build a future. A couple were merchants whose stores were replenished when heavily guarded wagons were able to reach the settlement. Then there were those drawn to the place because it was beyond the reach of the law. Some were hard-eyed men with no visible means of making a living. A few were there because the Confederacy was now conscripting soldiers rather than relying on volunteers, but exempting those who served in the Texas State Troops, also known as the Home Guard. Service in the Guard, for all its dangers, was preferable to being sent to the butchering grounds of the battlefields back East.

John's guard duties cut into his time at the ranch, but he did not mind. He never said so openly, but the pure thrill of the chase, and the exhilaration of battle with Indian raiders and the occasional white bandit, provided their own rewards.

Comanche and Kiowa raiders were constantly on the prowl in large bands now that there was no organized military force to keep them confined to reservations. Hardly a week went by that the Guard wasn't in pursuit of raiders or on scout. John was

mildly surprised there hadn't been more trouble with white renegades. There were enough of them about.

"John! John Selman!"

The call jolted John from his reverie. He glanced over his
shoulder. Charlie McIntire led a half-dozen riders at a fast trot,
their horses' hooves kicking up a small dust cloud.

"What is it, Charlie?"

"Better saddle up, John. We got us a horse thief to catch."

John scrambled down from his perch atop the skeleton of the
house. Tom had already gone into action, unhitching the team
from the picket wagon where Tom's roan and John's big bay were
pulling a day in harness. Saddles and weapons waited in the
wagon bed.

Fifteen minutes later Slim Gentry had picked up the trail of the
thief. John's dislike for Gentry grew every time he rode with the
man, but nobody could challenge Gentry's ability as a tracker.
And this was a clean trail to follow.

The captured thief knelt beneath a cottonwood tree, the shadow
of a noose drifting back and forth across a tear-streaked face
twisted in fear.

"Now I lay me down to sleep"—John winced at the words. The
thief was barely into his teens, and his mind had stopped growing
years ago—"The Lord is my shepherd, Jesus my savior—"

"Let's get it over with," Gentry snapped. "Hang the thieving
little bastard. I got chores back home."

John glowered at Gentry. The man really was mean as a snake,
and deadly—provided a man's back was turned. John was about
to call Gentry down when Charlie McIntire raised a hand.

"Wait a minute," McIntire said. He glanced around the circle
of men, then gestured toward the huddled youth. "I can't hang a
half-wit. Everybody here knows Jocko's got no more mind than a
six-year-old."

"What the hell difference does that make?" Gentry flicked the
rope. "He stole a horse and blanket. He deserves to hang same as
a man growed."

"It just ain't the same," Charlie said. A couple of other riders
nodded in silent agreement. John glanced at his younger brother.
He couldn't read Tom's eyes. The younger Selman stood expres-

sionless, as if it didn't matter to him. "John," Charlie said, "you the lieutenant. What's your feelin' about it?"

"You called it, Charlie. This boy doesn't know right from wrong. I've helped you men run down a few Indians and a white horse thief or two, and I'm not against a good healthy hanging for those who earn it. But I'm not going to be part of any mob that lynches this kid."

"Now I lay me down to sleep . . ."

"Shut up the praying a minute, Jocko," John said. "Why did you steal that horse?"

The boy hiccuped a sob. "I just wanted—wanted to ride. I got lost and scared. Weren't nobody—nobody usin' that horse. I didn't think nobody would mind. I wouldn't steal nothin', 'cause Jesus, he said it was wrong to steal."

Gentry cursed and started toward the boy. John let his hand drop to the pistol holstered at his side. "Get away from him, Gentry!"

Gentry stopped. He turned to face John, his own hand resting on his belt gun.

"You gonna stop me, Selman? You gonna shoot one of your own kind to save a hoss thief?"

"You're not one of my kind, Gentry. I've never hung a man yet who didn't deserve it." John's words were soft, the tone deadly. "I'll shoot you if I have to."

Gentry's defiance faded beneath John's steady glare. "I reckon you'd try, Selman. I don't wanna tangle with you just yet." Gentry's face flushed in anger, but raw fear showed in the small, close-set eyes. John struggled against the urge to draw his pistol and kill Gentry on the spot. It might save a lot of trouble down the road. Gentry finally shrugged and turned away. John knew the moment had passed, but he vowed to watch his back-trail when Gentry was around.

"The Lord is my—"

"Shut up, Jocko." John knelt beside the terrified youth. The boy was crying and pleading all at the same time. "Now, son, I know you meant no harm. But while we were off chasing you, thinking you were a real horse thief, what if Indians raided our homes and somebody got killed? How would you feel about that?"

The boy sobbed openly. "I never—never thought—about that."

John sighed, then turned to Charlie. "It's your horse he took, Charlie. I guess that makes it your call."

McIntire's forehead wrinkled in thought. "He's got to learn a lesson. Why don't we just whup him good, like one of our own?"

There was a general mutter of agreement. "Fair enough," John said. "Somebody lay a belt on him." At the corner of his vision he saw Gentry reach for his belt buckle. "Not you, Gentry," John warned. "I don't want him beaten to death, either." Gentry muttered a string of oaths, but didn't press the point.

John stepped alongside Tom. "Keep an eye on Gentry for me, Tom. If he goes for his gun, shoot the sonofabitch."

Tom half smiled and nodded.

John turned away, unwilling to watch the punishment of the half-wit. He fiddled with the cinch of his saddle and listened to the whop of leather against skin, the whimper of the boy. He tried to tell himself that at least he had helped save the kid's life. But it didn't help the taste in his mouth.

Finally, the sounds stopped. "All right," John said. "Boost him back onto that horse, and let's go home."

John Selman tamped a handful of mud into the final chink of the picket house in Fort Davis. He wiped the sweat from his brow and stepped back to look over his work.

It was impressive in size if not polished in workmanship, he conceded. The house contained a combination dining room and kitchen with a rock fireplace and chimney, a bedroom for the Widow Selman, a second for himself and Tom, and a third for the girls. The rooms weren't big, but they would provide some privacy.

"It's a good house, John," his mother said at his side.

He wrapped his arm around her shoulders in a brief hug. "It's not pretty, but it'll be warm in winter and cool in summer. Some day we'll build you a really fine place. Out of rock. Or maybe even brick, with cut-glass windows, real floors, and all the rooms you want."

The widow Selman smiled. "This is all I need, John Selman, and you better start thinking about a house for yourself and Edna deGraffenreid next. When are you going after that girl, anyway? You fiddle around too long, somebody else is going to have her in harness.''

The question floated a picture of Edna to the surface of John's mind—a slender oval face framed in dark hair, a gentle smile on full lips and reflected in quiet eyes. A woman worth the wait and all the work.

"Soon, Mother," John said. "A couple of weeks, maybe, no more. I have something to offer Edna now. A few head of cows and a little money make a man feel better about taking a wife." He sighed and smiled at the Widow Selman. "I don't see a thing to stand in the way now."

John Selman swabbed at the black powder residue in the breech of the Sharps. For all its good points, the rifle was prone to fouling; it had to be thoroughly cleaned after each use to make sure it functioned reliably and accurately. The Sharps had put down a prime young buck deer at dawn today, and now it demanded its own feeding.

At the hitch-rail outside, John's horse, saddled and with blanket roll and bags already tied in place for the long ride to Sherman, whickered softly, greeting other horses.

The back door swung open and Tom Selman stepped into the room, the skinning knife in his hand stained from butchering the deer under the Widow Selman's direction. She was particular about her venison cuts.

"Riders coming, John. Four of them. Soldiers." Tom tossed the knife on the counter, plucked his Springfield from its pegs with a blood-smeared hand, and strode to the single window overlooking the front yard.

John left the rifle on the table and slipped the Colt from its holster.

"Hello, the house!"

John toed the door open, his thumb on the hammer of the handgun. A cold hand clamped around his gut.

A Confederate Army corporal sat astride a rangy chestnut gelding. A double-barrel shotgun rested in the crook of his left arm. Behind the corporal were three other troopers, all nervous privates.

"John Henry Selman?"

John swung the door open. "I'm John Selman."

"Corporal Jennings, Fort Belnap. I have a warrant for your arrest on a charge of desertion from the Army of the Confederacy."

John glanced toward Tom and shook his head. The two Selmans might be able to put the soldiers down, but then the charge would be murder. That would bring more than four troopers. It wasn't worth the gamble. "Let it slide, Tom," he said, trying to keep his voice calm and even. *Dammit,* he thought, *why now? Another hour and I'd have been on my way to Sherman and Edna.* "Get Mother, Tom. I'll be wanting to say goodbye to her."

John lowered the pistol. "Let me get a few things. I'll not give you any trouble."

"I hope not, Mister Selman. I would hate to have to shoot you."

John surrendered his handgun. He heard the familiar footsteps of his mother at his back. The Widow Selman stepped alongside John and glanced at the soldiers. "I'll put some clothes together for you, John," she said.

The corporal stood in the doorway and watched as John gathered a few personal items and dropped them into a soft leather bag. His mother came from the bedroom, a small bundle under her arm. She embraced her son. John felt the cold steel of a pistol slip into the waistband of his trousers beneath his shirt.

"Take care of yourself, John," the Widow Selman said.

"You too, Mother." John took the bundle from her hand and held it against his belly. "Please get word to Edna that—that I'm sorry." He turned to his younger brother. "Watch over the family, Tom. I'll be all right."

John Selman turned to face the corporal. "Let's get on with it," he said.

They had ridden barely a mile from Fort Davis before John had sized up the four men. The three privates had little taste for the job at hand. The corporal was the dangerous one. *Patience, John,* he warned himself, *a lot can happen in forty miles; you just have to pick your spot.* He rode with a slight slump, letting the folds of his shirt disguise the stubby hideout weapon in his waistband. He recognized it from the shape and feel of it against his skin. His father's ancient Wesson and Leavitt side-hammer model, thirty-one caliber, barrel cut down to little more than three inches. Not a powerful gun, but adequate at close range.

By the time the sun was overhead, John had gained the confidence of the privates, laughing and joking. Corporal Jennings rode in front, shotgun at the ready. Twice the corporal turned and scowled at the troopers flanking John. The third time he turned and barked an order: "No talking with the prisoner!"

Jennings called the noon camp in a clump of cottonwoods alongside a spring in a creek fifteen miles east-northeast of Fort Davis. The corporal told the trooper named Stanford to guard the prisoner; the two other privates leaned their rifles against a tree, apparently more concerned about a biscuit and a few slices of bacon than about the deserter. Jennings put his shotgun aside and pulled his own mess kit from the knapsack tied to his saddle.

John sensed he wasn't likely to get another opportunity like this.

"Corporal Jennings?" John kept his voice light, the tone conversational.

"Yes?"

"Nature calls."

Jennings nodded toward the trooper guarding John. "Stanford, keep a sharp eye on Selman. Mind your step. Can't trust a deserter."

Stanford followed a step behind John, rifle in the crook of an elbow, as the two strode casually toward the edge of the clearing.

"What's the latest on the war, Stanford? We don't get much news out this way."

Stanford's brow wrinkled. "Not good. The Yankees got all the men, guns, and gunpowder they need. We got cotton and watermelon." The trooper spat. "Damn hard to knock out a battery of six-pounders with a watermelon."

"Suspected as much." The two were out of sight of the camp now in the cover of the trees. John turned his back to Stanford and pretended to fiddle with the buttons of his trousers. His hand closed around the butt of the revolver. "Where you from, Stanford?"

"Virginia. Shenandoah Valley. Pretty country this time—" His drawl ended in a sharp intake of breath as John turned, the cocked pistol pointed between Stanford's eyes.

"Just stand easy, soldier," John said, his voice low. "I don't want to have to hurt you. Now, real easy—take your thumbnail and flip the cap off the nipple of that Springfield."

Stanford did as he was told. The rifle was now useless. "Now we walk back to camp, side by side," John said. "I'll have the pistol in your back, so act like nothing's wrong."

As the two men entered the clearing, John stepped from Stanford's side and pointed the muzzle of the handgun toward the corporal.

"Corporal Jennings, this is as far as I go." John saw the corporal twitch in momentary surprise, then stab a hand toward the shotgun lying near his side. "Don't try it, Jennings," he warned.

The corporal froze, his fingertips resting on the shotgun. There was no way he could lift the weapon, cock it, and fire before a pistol ball tore through him, and he knew it. John could see the fear build in the corporal's eyes.

"Now, fellows," John said, "I haven't lived twenty-some years just to wind up in a Confederate stockade somewhere. Everybody stay nice and calm and nobody'll get hurt. Unbuckle the sidearms and toss them over this way."

The soldiers did as they were told. John collected the belts, tied them to the troopers' saddles, then thrust the Springfields into saddle boots. He retrieved his own Army Colt and gunbelt and Jennings's shotgun, then necked the Army mounts together with picket rope. He mounted his bay and wrapped the picket rope around the saddle horn.

"Gentlemen," he said, "I'll not leave a man afoot and unarmed in Indian country." He waved the muzzle of the hideout gun toward the south. "When I ride out, follow this creek about a quarter mile until you see a clump of rocks halfway up the side of a hill. There's a pinoak tree that's been hit by lightning. I'll leave your handguns and ammunition there. A couple of miles further down you'll find your horses and long guns. I'll have to keep one of the Springfields and an ammunition pouch for my own use. Fair enough?"

The trooper named Stanford swallowed and nodded. His face

was the color of flour gravy. The corporal glared at John. "Selman, nobody does this to me. Especially a damn coward."

John's gaze locked on Jennings's face. "Corporal, it's not a good idea to make a man mad when he's holding a cocked pistol on your gut. If you're stupid enough to come after me, fine. Or you can save yourself a ride and we'll settle it right now."

The angry flush drained from the corporal's face. Jennings's gaze dropped under John's cold stare. John knew he had won. He kneed the bay around and put the animal into a trot toward the south.

TWO

Fort Davis
Summer 1865

Tom Selman pulled his slicker tighter against the driving rain and cursed the elements.

Five more head of Selman stock lost to rustlers, the day-old tracks washed away by the sudden thunderstorm. He pounded a clenched fist into the saddle horn. *Dammit, at this rate we won't have a cow left by winter.* But this time, at least, he had something to show for his efforts. One of the rustlers rode a horse with a turned-out right forefoot. The horse had a habit of dragging that foot when it walked; the tip of the hoof was worn almost square. It was a distinctive track. And he had a good idea whose horse it was. Slim Gentry's.

The little thief will pay for this, Tom promised himself. It would have saved a lot of trouble and several head of Four Clubs cattle if John had shot Gentry the day they faced off over hanging the half-wit. Tom suspected Gentry was behind John's arrest, and now he had a connection between Gentry and the missing Selman cattle. *By God, Gentry,* Tom vowed, *you'll find out there's more than one Selman to deal with.* He turned his roan gelding back toward Fort Davis.

The summer storm had slowed to a drizzle two hours later as Tom reined his mount into the muddy main street of the Clear Fork settlement. A dozen yards away, three horses stood hip-shot at the rail before Bartlett's half house, half saloon. One of them was Slim Gentry's dun gelding.

Tom dismounted and lifted the dun's right forefoot. The toe of the hoof was worn off almost square. It was a perfect match to the tracks he had followed before the storm. Tom's fingers trembled in a fresh surge of rage as he released the dun's hoof. He stepped through the sucking mud and pushed open the door of Bartlett's saloon.

Gentry and another rider, a man known only as Gordy, stood at the bar, backs to the door and whiskey glasses in hand. Tom slipped his Navy thirty-six from its holster.

"Gentry!"

The slender figure at the bar straightened, then turned slowly toward Tom. Thin brows rose above close-set eyes as Gentry saw the pistol in Tom's fist. "Well, I'll be fresh damned," Gentry said. "It's the Selman whelp. And he's got himself a little *pistole.*" Gentry smirked. "Better be careful, sonny. You might hurt your-self."

"Where were you yesterday, Gentry?"

Gentry leaned against the bar. "What the hell business is it of yours?"

"Cow business. Three riders stole some Selman stock. One of the rustlers was riding your horse. I'm curious about who that might've been, Gentry."

Gentry's eyes narrowed. "That's serious talk for a wet-behind-the-ears kid to make, Tom Selman. Sort of thing that could get you killed. You better be hoss enough to back up that talk."

"I'm hoss enough." At the corner of his vision Tom saw the man called Gordy edge away from Gentry and drop his hand to his waistband. Tom raised the Navy. "Hold it right there, Gordy. I'll take you down just like your friend here." Gordy raised both hands, palm out. Tom wondered why the man was smiling. He turned his attention back to Gentry. "I'm calling your hand, Gentry. Let's get this—" Tom's challenge ended in a blast of white light as something slammed into the side of his head. His hand went numb. He felt the pistol drop to the floor, his arms pinned to his side by a powerful grip. He struggled to refocus his eyes, and fought to breathe through the pressure against his ribs.

Slim Gentry took two steps forward and drove a fist into Tom's belly, then slugged him, left and right, hard in the face. Tom felt the skin rip on his cheek. A roaring sound filled his head; he thought he heard a yell from a great distance just before the barrel of Gentry's gun slammed into the side of his head. Then

Tom felt himself sliding down a long, slippery hillside into darkness.

Waco, Texas

John Selman lashed the final pole into place on the new holding pens on the north side of the Simms Ranch east of Waco, and wiped a soggy sleeve over the sweat that trickled from beneath his hatband.

Carl Simms was a good man to work for, even if he did get his money's worth from the help. He didn't ask a lot of foolish questions like where a man was from and where he was headed. Simms just wanted to know if a man would work.

John flexed the aching muscles in his shoulders. The work seemed a lot harder when it wasn't for yourself, he thought. But life was still a damn sight easier here than it would be in some stockade.

He reached for the burlap-wrapped water jug in the shadow of a gatepost and let his thoughts drift once more to North Texas and home. The cattle most likely were scattered now. Tom was good at many things, but riding drift on a herd wasn't one of them. Lord only knows, he thought, how many of them might have been stolen since he had ridden away. He could only hope that some of the Four Clubs herd he had worked so hard to build still were grazing the Brazos country grass.

John worried some about his family. The Widow Selman was a competent and tough woman, though, and they had good neighbors if real trouble came along. Maybe Tom had filled his place as the breadwinner. John tried not to think of Edna. That was too painful a memory.

He lowered the water jug and picked up his rifle as a horseman topped the ridge a hundred yards to the south. The rider wasn't one of Simms's hands. John cocked the old Army Springfield and waited as the rider neared. The man wore the faded butternut brown of the Confederate cavalry. John raised the rifle as he recognized the soldier. The last time he had seen him had been over the barrel of an old thirty-one-caliber pistol.

"That's close enough, Private Stanford," he called.

The horseman checked his mount, then raised both hands, palms toward John. "Selman? John Selman?"

"Nobody here knows me by that name, Stanford. State your business."

"I've got a message for you. From the Widow Selman."

John lowered the muzzle of the Springfield. "Ride on in," he said, "but keep your hands where I can see them."

Stanford dismounted and looped the reins over a corral pole. "Your old company's been disbanded, Selman. My outfit, too. We're both off the cannon-fodder hook." Stanford glanced at the water jug and licked his lips. "The long of it is that the Confederacy is falling apart. The short of it is that the warrant for you has been dropped. The Army of the Confederacy is no longer interested in having your hide nailed to the barn door."

John studied the young man's sunburned face, the expression in the dark eyes. If Stanford were lying, John decided, he was a master of the art.

"Which means?"

"Which means you can go home, John Selman. Hell, I'm headed home myself." Stanford's grin was without mirth. "If there's anything left of the Shenandoah Valley after the Yankees are finished with it."

John lowered the hammer of the Springfield and nodded toward the water container. "Help yourself, Stanford." He waited until the young soldier drank and recorked the jug. "How did you find me?"

"When the charges were dropped, I went to see your mother, to let her know. She told me you had written her a couple of times, that you were using the name Graham and working on a ranch near Waco. Wasn't that hard." Stanford leaned against a fence post and wiped perspiration from his brow.

"Why should you give a tinker's damn about me, Stanford?"

The young ex-soldier sighed. "I guess I felt like I owed you one. You could have killed us all out there, but you didn't. You could have taken the horses and left us afoot, taken the guns and left us to God knows what, and you didn't. I wanted to square accounts before I leave this part of the country." Stanford grinned. The smile seemed genuine. "Besides, your mother gave me thirty dollars in real American silver—not Confederate paper —to find you. That's my going-home money."

John sat silent for a moment, scratching at the mental itch until the tickle went away. "I believe you, Stanford. It's the best news I've had in weeks."

Stanford pushed himself away from the corral fence. "One more thing, Selman. There's a man in Fort Davis doesn't seem to like you much. Name's Gentry. He's the one who told the captain at Camp Cooper you were a deserter. He also pistol-whipped your brother pretty bad a few weeks back. Turk Bartlett broke it up before Gentry could do too much damage."

John flexed his left hand into a fist. "What happened? Is Tom all right?"

"Got his pride hurt worse than anything else. No permanent physical damage. As to what set it off, nobody seems too anxious to talk, Tom included. Gentry hasn't been seen since Bartlett pulled him off Tom and booted him out of the saloon."

Stanford swung into the saddle. "Was I you, John Selman, I'd watch my back." The ex-Confederate soldier raised a hand in farewell. "It's a long way to Virginia. I'd best be moving on. Good luck, Selman."

"Good luck to you, Stanford. I'll keep my powder dry, and thanks for the warning."

John watched the Virginian ride away, his emotions torn between joy at going home and worry over Tom and the Gentry affair.

Finally, a smile pushed through the dirt on his face. *First thing I do when I get home,* he promised himself, *is shave off this blasted beard; itches like the devil in the summertime. Then I'm going for Edna.*

Fort Davis

Mrs. John Selman, until a few weeks ago Miss Edna deGraffenreid of Sherman, wrapped both hands around her new husband's upper left arm as the buggy creaked around the final bend in the road leading to the Selman family's picket home.

John reined in the sorrel buggy horse a couple of hundred

yards from the house. "I hope it isn't too much a disappointment to you, Edna." Edna heard the apology in her husband's voice. "It isn't much. But one day I'll build you a fine home. With hardwood floors and a flower garden or two."

Edna squeezed his bicep. "Hardwood floors don't make a home, John. I think it's beautiful. It's our home. Any woman who would ask for more is a fool."

John tapped the reins against the sorrel's rump and smiled as the buggy jolted into motion. He glanced at the young woman at his side. Her slender face was serene, tiny laugh wrinkles at the corners of her eyes reflecting her ready smile. A gentle and sensitive woman. John hoped she wasn't too gentle and sensitive for the frontier. The Clear Fork country was hard on horses and women.

Edna's steady optimism was a soothing counterpoint to the bleak moods that John Selman sometimes endured but could not explain. He never doubted that she would be a good wife and mother.

John sighed, contented. Now he had everything a man could want—or at least a good start on it.

John Selman stood at the end of the receiving line outside the small church, his wife and mother chatting quietly as they waited for the circuit preacher to make his way to them.

The Reverend C. C. Slaughter, Baptist minister and Indian fighter, was a big man, over six feet tall with a voice as powerful as his heavy shoulders and a way of persuading folks to follow The Word. The reverend was already something of a legend on the frontier, and even without his mother's and wife's urgings John might have forgone a Sunday morning's work to hear Slaughter rail against sin.

Slaughter's ragings against Old Scratch were a form of entertainment as well as spiritual inspiration to the folks on the frontier. John had heard it said that people would rather sleep through a Comanche raid than miss one of Slaughter's tussles with Satan. *Somebody really ought to speak up for Satan once in a while,* John mused. *He sure keeps a lot of folks occupied around here.*

Slaughter had performed the ceremony when Lucinda Selman married Todd Willet, and frequently stayed at the Widow

Selman's home during his swings through Fort Davis. He accepted the compliments on his sermon of the morning, then reached for John's hand. "Well, Mister Selman. It's a pleasure true to have you among the flock this morning. Are you ready to make that final step and be baptized, as has your mother?"

John smiled at the preacher. At the same time he noted the bulge beneath Slaughter's frock coat. The parson was seldom without his revolver, even during church services. John shook his head.

"Not yet, Reverend. You can bedevil hell out of Old Satan, sure enough, but the water in the Clear Fork is a touch on the cool side for this sinner's liking."

There was an obvious twinkle in Slaughter's eyes. "I'll get your soul on the right side of the Jordan River yet, John Selman. In the meantime, the Lord bless and keep you and yours. You'll be staying for the dinner? The ladies have laid out quite a spread."

The clatter of horse's hooves approaching at a lope interrupted the conversation. Tom Selman pulled his sorrel to a sliding stop before John.

"They hit us again, John," Tom said. "Three of them. Took six head of stock, headed north not more than four, five hours ago. The tracks say Gentry's dun is one of the horses."

"I'll get my horse." John turned toward the buggy where his saddled horse switched flies behind the tailgate. C. C. Slaughter followed, and leaned against the buggy as John tugged the cinches tight.

"Rustlers, eh?" Slaughter's expression turned grim. "I heard someone say it's getting so a rancher can't buy stock fast enough to meet the demands of rustlers around here. If you'd like some help"—the preacher patted the bulge beneath his coat—"just let me get my horse."

"Thanks for the offer, Reverend, but we each have flocks to tend. At the moment, yours is bigger than mine."

John felt a tug at his arm. "John, please. Take some more men with you—" Edna's eyes were wide, her fear obvious in the soft brown irises. The Widow Selman stood at Edna's side.

"No, Edna. Tom and I can stomp our own snakes."

"Dammit, John, hurry up!" Impatience clipped Tom's words.

"We'll have no cursing before the house of God, Tom," the

Widow Selman snapped. Then her tone softened. "Take care, both of you. "Cows we can replace. We haven't any spare Selmans."

John swung into the saddle and nodded to his brother. "Lead the way, Tom. Let's get our cows back."

Reverend Slaughter watched as John and Tom Selman kneed their horses into an easy, ground-covering trot. "Blast it," he muttered under his breath. "Getting to where a man of the cloth can't have any real fun anymore." He remembered the look in John Selman's pale blue eyes and the tight, controlled rage on the face of young Tom. Slaughter reminded himself to offer up a prayer for the hunters. He wouldn't pray for the hunted. As far as C. C. Slaughter was concerned, a man who stole another man's cows had no soul to begin with.

John heard the familiar bawl of the brindle cow, one of the first slicks he had caught, at the same time his nostrils caught the faint scent of wood smoke. These three rustlers were pretty casual about their trade, he thought. They had left a track a ten-year-old could follow.

He raised a clenched fist to Tom and pointed toward the grove of cottonwoods on the bank of the Brazos River tributary known as Ketchum Creek. Tom nodded, pointed to his chest, and waved toward the right.

The Selman brothers ground-hitched their mounts and checked their weapons one final time. Tom melted from sight into the low scrub brush. John made his way toward the cottonwoods, placing his feet with care and keeping the light breeze in his face. The smell of burning wood grew stronger. John shifted the Sharps to his left hand and palmed the Colt. He could hear voices now, the words muted by the thicket and the heavy air.

He parted the branches at the edge of a clearing in the middle of the cottonwood grove. A dozen yards away Slim Gentry and the man called Gordy crouched by a small fire, an L-shaped running iron heating in the flames. The third rustler, a stranger to John, stood with the horses at the far side of the clearing. All three carried holstered handguns, their rifles still in saddle scabbards.

The brindle cow struggled against the tie-down ropes and

bellowed again. Beyond the clearing another cow bawled an answer. The stolen animals, John guessed, were probably necked together or hobbled to keep them from running while the iron heated. A lariat rope lay slack near the brindle's head.

John waited, listening. The chirr of a quail sounded to his right. He did not need to look. Tom would be in position. John concentrated on the two men at the fire.

"By God, Gordy," Gentry punctuated the comment with a grin, "a few more head and we'll have John Selman and that whelp of a brother of his bled near to death. Never thought a man could make easy money and get even at the same time."

John could not make out the younger man's reply.

"And when John Selman's lost damn near everything, I finish it. First, that new wife of his." Gentry chuckled aloud. "About time she knew what a real man was. Then I'll put Selman in my sights, face-to-face. I'm lookin' forward to that, I tell you—"

John stepped into the clearing.

"You can stop looking, Gentry," he said.

Gentry glanced up, startled. The color drained from his face. Then he yelped a curse and stabbed a hand to the pistol at his belt.

John shot him in the belly. Gentry staggered backward, mouth open but making no sound. The half-drawn handgun tumbled into the dust as he fell. Out of the corner of his eye, John saw the rustler holding the horses sweep a rifle from a scabbard, then tumble backward as the heavy blast of Tom's Springfield thundered through the clearing. John swung the muzzle of his Colt toward Gordy.

The man raised his hands. "Don't shoot! For Christ's sake, don't kill me! This was Gentry's doing, not mine—"

Tom stepped into view, his Navy Colt in his hand.

"This the one helped Gentry pistol-whip you, Tom?"

Tom lifted his handgun and fired. Gordy's head snapped back as the soft lead ball slammed into his skull just above his eyes. He was dead before he hit the ground. *Guess I got my answer,* John thought. He glanced at Tom. His brother's lips twisted into a half smile. *Damn, he's just killed a man—and enjoyed it.* John pushed the thought away. Tom had earned the right.

John put the dead man from his mind and turned toward Gentry. The wounded man struggled to a sitting position, arms wrapped around his torn midsection, eyes wide in pain and terror. "Help—help me. I'm—gut-shot."

John nodded casually. "I know. That's what I had in mind." He kicked the fallen handgun beyond Gentry's reach.

"Get me—to doc—" Gentry's voice failed as agony twisted his narrow face. He really did look like a possum, John thought. A possum with its tail caught in a big rat trap.

"Gonna die—without help—hurtin' real bad—"

"We'll help, Gentry. Tom and I. You remember my brother, I expect." John squatted before the wounded man, Tom at his side. Raw terror flared through the pain in Gentry's eyes. John knew why. He had seen Tom's expression before, in the eyes of a wolf stalking a crippled steer. "Before we help you, Gentry," John said, "I want to know how many other cows of mine you stole. And where they are."

"McLochlin." Gentry's voice was a hoarse croak. "Sold 'em— McLochlin. Fifteen—twenty head."

John swore softly. J. D. McLochlin's ranch was ten miles north of the Brazos. McLochlin had a half-dozen hands, all as good with guns as they were with cattle. But that was a different cat up another tree.

"God, Selman—I—I'm hurtin'—real bad."

John turned to Tom. "What about it, Tom?"

Tom spat. "Let's hang the little bastard and be done with it." Tom rose, strode to Gentry's horse, and led the animal back to the downed man. John lifted Gentry to his feet and almost threw him onto the horse. Gentry screamed in a fresh wave of agony and sagged over the saddle horn.

John retrieved the lariat rope from where it lay beside the brindle cow. He led Gentry's horse to a nearby cottonwood, tossed the loop end of the rope over a limb, and tied the other end firm to the trunk.

Gentry raised his head. His pain-glazed eyes widened in a wash of terror. "What—what—"

Tom dropped the loop of the rope over Gentry's neck.

"No—for God's sake—"

John slapped Gentry's horse on the rump. The animal bolted.

Gentry dropped a couple of feet before the weight of his body snapped the rope taught.

John slipped a knife from his belt and cut the tie ropes from the brindle cow. She struggled for a moment, got her feet under her, and stood with a snort. She swung her head as if to charge, then started to trot south, back toward her home range.

John glanced at Gentry. The fall hadn't broken his neck. The rustler's fingers clawed at the noose buried in his flesh, legs flailing. His eyes bulged in the purple face and a stain spread at his crotch. The fingers fell away from his neck.

Tom leaned against the trunk of the tree, relaxed and smiling, and watched as Gentry's body finally went limp and twisted slowly at the end of the rope.

"Feel better about it now, Tom?" John asked.

"A lot better." Tom nodded toward the bodies in the clearing. "So what do we do with them?"

"Leave them where they are. Gentry, too."

Ten minutes later Tom and John herded the Four Clubs cattle back toward home range.

"What about McLochlin?" Tom asked.

"We'll call on him tomorrow. For now we've got to make sure the cattle make it back home. Besides, it's getting on toward supper time." John reined his horse after the Four Clubs cattle. McLochlin could wait until morning. He was mildly surprised to hear Tom whistling, off-key, "When the Roll Is Called Up Yonder."

J. D. McLochlin leaned his stocky body against a porch pole of the sturdy log-and-stone ranch house and met the cool, level gaze of the rider on the big bay facing him. Two McLochlin riders stood at each end of the porch, hands never far from the revolvers at their sides.

"Mister Selman," McLochlin said, "you must have bigger *cojones* than a prime Mexican stud horse." The rancher's words carried the soft burr of his native Scotland. "It takes either a brave man or a fool to ride onto a man's ranch and accuse him of dealing in stolen cattle. If I were to give the word, these men would shoot you into several small pieces for such an insult."

John Selman leaned forward, right forearm resting casually

across the wide horn of his Mexican-made saddle, his left hand still holding the reins. A slight smile lifted the corners of his mustache. "Well, Mister McLochlin, I never considered myself a brave man. And I don't believe a fool would have left his younger brother with a buffalo gun in those trees just yonder."

One of the McLochlin men glanced warily at the clump of cottonwoods a hundred yards distant.

John let his right hand fall to his thigh near the butt of the Colt revolver. "You give that word to your riders, Mister McLochlin, and the first thing that happens is a fifty-two-caliber Sharps slug takes your heart out." John's tone was flat, matter-of-fact. "Messy thing, a Sharps. Makes a God-awful hole. Now, I just came to talk. But if you want shooting instead, I suppose we can accommodate you."

McLochlin's scowl cracked, and slowly gave way to a grin. "By God, Selman, I'd not play poker with the likes of you. I'll sure not call your hand, for this might be no bluff. No harm in a little conversation." The scowl returned. "Mind you, lad, I don't take to being called a thief."

"I didn't say you were, Mister McLochlin. I'm just telling you what was told to me. That there might be some of my cattle on your range. The man who said it is known to be a bald-faced liar as well as a thief. If I knew for a fact you were responsible for anyone rustling my stock, I'd have shot you first and found the cows later. At the moment I'm just interested in how I can get my cattle back. *If* they're here."

McLochlin scratched the stubble on his sunburned cheek. He didn't doubt for a moment that Selman held all the aces; he could almost feel the front sight of a hidden Sharps pressing into the left pocket of his shirt. It wasn't particularly comfortable. He shrugged.

"Very well, Mister Selman. I want you to understand first that I've never knowingly purchased any stolen cattle."

The man on the bay tilted his head. "I've no reason to doubt your word, Mister McLochlin."

McLochlin felt the tension begin to ease. "Mister Selman, if any of your cattle are on this ranch, I will return them and apologize." The rancher turned to the man at his right. "Everett, bring my horse around. You and Daley come with me and Mister Selman to scout the herds. We will gather any cattle he claims as his, branded or not, and help him trail them back to his ranch."

"Sounds fair, Mister McLochlin," John said. "And if we find any of my cows here, I'll pay back whatever amount those rustlers did you out of."

McLochlin took the reins of a lanky sorrel gelding from the rider called Everett and mounted. "No need. If I bought stolen cattle it was my own fault, and a man admits his mistakes. And if those men you describe show up around here, I promise they will steal no more cattle."

Selman smiled, but McLochlin noted there was no mirth in the gesture. Selman turned in the saddle and waved toward the trees. Moments later a young man rode into view, a heavy Sharps cradled in his arms and a Springfield carbine in the saddle boot. McLochlin studied the younger man. He had the same cold set to the eyes, the same strong jawline, as John Selman.

"Mister McLochlin, my brother Tom."

The rancher nodded a greeting. Tom Selman made no effort to return the gesture. McLochlin touched spurs to the sorrel. As they rode, McLochlin raised his opinion of John Selman another notch. Selman showed his trust by riding alongside McLochlin at the head of the group of riders, and his caution by having his brother bring up the rear. Any unexpected move by a McLochlin rider would bring the Sharps into play. A deadly pair, McLochlin concluded.

McLochlin knew there was no Selman stock on his ranch this day. The handful of cattle wearing the Four Clubs brand were long gone from McLochlin range, headed north on the trail to Dodge City. There was no doubt in McLochlin's mind that Gentry and those two friends of his would spread no loose talk now.

The Scot prided himself in his ability to turn almost any situation to his own advantage. He could read men and play them like a hundred-dollar fiddle. The Selmans could be useful in the near future. Soon, big ranchers like himself would need the services of men like the Selman brothers to help protect their herds and their land. At that time such men would be beyond price. Now he had the chance to gain their trust.

The sun was low in the west when the horsemen returned. The

Selmans declined McLochlin's offer of supper and a drink. The Scot breathed a silent sigh of relief as the two rode from sight.

McLochlin turned to his foreman. "Everett, tomorrow I want you to scout the country between here and Fort Davis. Look for buzzards. I think you'll find the remains of Mister Slim Gentry and his *compadres* where you find the birds." McLochlin sighed. "Bury the bodies well. I want no trace left that those men ever set foot on McLochlin Land & Cattle Company soil."

The Scot paused to fill and light his pipe before going in for supper and a whiskey. Gentry had almost brought him more grief than livestock. But he had turned a potential problem into an advantage. He had gained a small measure of confidence from the Selmans today.

J. D. McLochlin exhaled a cloud of blue smoke. It was, all things considered, an excellent trade.

Fort Davis
May 1867

It seemed to Edna Selman that the entire population along the Clear Fork of the Brazos had come to pay their last respects to the Widow Selman.

Outside the small church, Edna dabbed at the tears which trickled down her cheeks and let herself be embraced yet again. "She was a fine woman, Edna." Katie Smith's own eyes were red with grief. "If there's solace to be found, it's that she went peacefully and without pain."

Edna returned the comforting hug. "Katie, I want you to know how much we appreciate your coming, and your being with Mother Selman when she—passed on. I know it meant a great deal to her, having such a good friend at her side."

Katie Smith took both Edna's hands in her own. "We all share your loss, Edna," she said. "I'll never forget the time she rode all night to come to us when my little girl was sick. I don't believe my girl would have lived without her. The Widow Selman just refused to let her give in to the fever and the pain."

Edna had heard many similar stories during the long two days before the funeral service, and even during the eulogy. "That was like her, Katie. She once told me a strong person could spit in the eye of death and then get out of bed to give the devil a boot in the backside. Even in her last few hours her concern was not her own weakness and suffering. She kept praying for John and me—to conceive a child."

Katie Smith gave Edna's shoulders a final squeeze. "I wouldn't put it past her to will such a thing into being, Edna. Even from the Hereafter."

Mrs. Smith moved on to embrace John, standing stiff and erect at Edna's side. Edna glanced at her husband. He had cried last night, silent tears in the solitude of the predawn darkness. It was the only time she had ever known John Selman to shed tears. Even now she could see the pain in his pale blue eyes.

Young Tom, on the other hand, displayed no signs of grief. He remained as stoic as ever. That was Tom's way, she knew. Anger, pain, loss, fear, love, embarrassment, frustration—all were held back from public view behind an impenetrable wall of pride and cold distance. Edna feared it would eat away at Tom until one day the pain built into a blind rage. She was forced to admit to herself that, deep inside, she was somewhat afraid of Tom Selman. Not of what he was, but of what he could become.

The receiving line thinned. A few moments later the plain pine coffin in which the Widow Selman rested was borne from the church to the black funeral wagon for the trip to the waiting grave on a knoll a few hundred yards from the bank of the Clear Fork.

As the coffin was lowered, Edna realized for the first time that the Widow Selman's duties had now been handed to another generation. To her. The knowledge lay heavy. *I'll never be as strong as she was,* Edna thought. *I can't hold this family together the way she did.*

THREE

Fort Griffin, Texas
February 1871

The wind gusted against the small three-room picket home on the banks of Tecumseh Creek. Pellets of sleet ticked against the north wall. The back door creaked with the gusts, keeping time with the faint scrape of Edna Selman's rocking chair.

John Selman sat at the dinner table, the pencil stub in his hand scratching from time to time as he updated the tally book. The last four winters had aged John beyond his thirty-two years, Edna thought. His dark hair was now streaked with gray, his face lined and weathered by sun and wind almost to the color of oiled leather.

The last few years, she conceded, would have aged any man. It had been that day on the Staked Plains that almost broke John's spirit.

The move to New Mexico had been a disaster. The promised land of better range and ready markets for their cattle and horses had been more like purgatory, dashing the hopes and plans of both John Selman and Edna's brother Jasper. It had cost them everything except their lives. Even that had been a near miss.

Edna still shuddered at the memory of the Indian raid, the emptiness in John's eyes and the sag of his shoulders, as they stood side by side in the smoldering wreckage of the wagon that had carried most of their worldly goods. They had fought off the Kiowa in that brief and bloody clash, but the raiding party had escaped with their cattle and horses, leaving the Selmans and Jasper all but destitute.

The months that followed were painful. John would come

home at night exhausted from a day of manual labor—grubbing brush from the crusty New Mexico soil, building corrals, or branding another man's cows. His efforts yielded a handful of coins a week, but his family had never gone hungry or cold. Finally he had been able to purchase a few head of steers. A fresh start.

They had come home. To Texas.

Their original home at Fort Davis no longer existed. It had crumbled with the rest of the community. Only the two half-built watchtowers still stood, stark reminders of the failed hopes of a town that once was home to more than a hundred people. The open range they had originally claimed was now grazed by other brands, mostly the ML of the McLaughlin herd. So the Selmans had settled near Fort Griffin, fifteen miles from their first home on the Clear Fork of the Brazos.

John sold the steers and used the money to buy a few mother cows. He and Tom were in the saddle from before dawn until after dark, catching and branding the wild cattle John called slicks. John chose the stock with care, and the herd began to grow. Sometimes Edna was startled to realize it had grown so quickly. She had heard rumors that others questioned the rapid expansion of what had become known as the Selman Red Herd, after John's penchant for red cattle. Edna tried to ignore the rumors, but they remained a constant source of worry. In this wild country rumors had a way of becoming truth.

At her side, five-month-old William Selman whimpered in his cradle. Edna knew the mewing was a preliminary to the full-blown cry of a hungry infant. The baby's fussing triggered an ache in Edna's over-full breasts. *Now I know what the milk cow feels like when it's past milking time,* she thought.

Despite the setbacks, Edna told herself, they had been twice-blessed. The final prayers of the Widow Selman had been answered two years ago with the birth of Henry, and now with William. Henry, the rambunctious one, was busy gathering chips from the kindling box by the stone fireplace and stowing them in his father's work boots as they dried on the hearth.

The hard times had not changed John's affection for Henry or William, or for his wife. Grimy, sweaty, and dog-tired, he always had a cheerful greeting and a hug for Edna and the children.

William had worked himself up to a full boil.

John glanced up and half smiled. "Time to feed the stock, girl," he said. He closed the tally book and put the pencil aside.

Edna picked up the baby, unbuttoned her dress, and sighed in contentment and relief as the child nuzzled her breast.

John turned and swept Henry into his lap. The toddler babbled something resembling a sentence. Small fingers probed his father's shirt pocket and found the prize—a pair of cartridges for John's new Henry forty-four-forty rifle. As the two played some sort of game with the cartridges—a game that Edna would never understand—she found herself wondering if their first son had been named for his father or for the new repeating rifle on its pegs beside the door. John's old Sharps rested on its own rack alongside the newer weapon, still potent in retirement.

Young Henry soon tired of the game, climbed from his father's lap, and scooted under the table to prowl among the forest of chair legs.

John rose, strode across the room, and placed a hand on his wife's shoulder. "Edna, it's time you had a proper house. We can afford it now."

"But John, the expense—"

John silenced her protest with a kiss on her cheek. "You've earned it, girl. We'll build across the creek, and we'll build it of decent timber and stone. A permanent house with lots of rooms. A home worthy of a good wife and a good mother. Tom and I'll start on it when the weather clears and have it finished by midsummer."

"John, I—"

"Hush, girl. A man has a right to give his wife an anniversary present." He gave her shoulder a final squeeze, shrugged into a heavy bearskin coat, and reached for his rifle.

"Oh, John. Do you really *have* to go out in weather like this?"

John paused, his hand on the door latch. "Cattle aren't very smart, Edna. There's always a few head that won't stay in the cover of the river breaks. If we don't turn them back they'll drift halfway to Mexico in this storm."

Edna lifted the baby to her shoulder, patted the child's back, and smiled at John. "I'll keep your supper warm for you. And I'll put the kids to bed early tonight."

Fort Griffin
Late Summer 1873

John Selman rode at a slow walk down to the community known as The Flats below Fort Griffin, nodding now and then to an acquaintance. The sun was barely past its high point, but already The Flats was awake and moving in a high lope. Hitch-rails before the ramshackle saloons were crowded with saddled horses, a smattering of wagons, and an occasional surrey or buggy. Hitching posts outside the whorehouses were equally crowded. John counted eight different brands on the hips of horses tied before The Flats' most popular sporting house.

Now and then the whoop of a drunken cowboy or buffalo hunter sounded through the general din of a busy street.

The rapid growth of The Flats had not taken John by surprise. The community had sprung into existence almost before the troops, mostly black soldiers commanded by white officers, had settled into their sparse quarters in the post above. A few legitimate merchants promptly erected shops to supply the needs of the fort. Businesses which catered to the physical needs of the soldiers had beaten the merchants there.

It was a town without law. Where the man with the biggest gun and best aim was most always in the right. And as the reputation of The Flats spread through the Texas frontier, a growing number of men on the east side of the law came west to the Fort Griffin country.

John Selman felt completely at home in The Flats.

He enjoyed the sounds and the smells of the town, the challenge of a good poker game. He had many friends—and a few enemies as well—in Fort Griffin. And for the first time in years, he didn't have to worry about every dollar he spent.

The Four Clubs cattle herd thrived on the lush grass and clear water along the river. The Selman family had also grown. Margaretta was almost a year old now, the image of her mother. Sons were a man's joy, he thought, but there was something special about a daughter.

John found a vacant spot at a hitch-rail and dismounted at Conner's Emporium, the town's best-equipped general store. He slipped his Henry from the saddle boot. There were those in The Flats who found it easier to steal something than to work for it, and good rifles left unattended were easy targets. John was about to enter the store when a familiar figure in the crowd along the street caught his eye.

"Pete!" he called out. "King James Peter Wolfpelt!"

The stocky Tonkawa turned, a broad grin slashing the wide bronze face. Whiskey Pete was showing a considerable paunch now, John noted, and it seemed that the Tonkawa had remained successful in avoiding an excess of bathwater since the Arroyo Blanco fight so many years ago.

Pete extended a hand. "John Selman. I'll be damned. Figured your hair'd be on some Comanche war lance by now."

"Been lucky, Pete. What brings you to this sin pit of the Plains?"

The brown eyes twinkled. "Just doin' what I do best, John. Huntin' Comanch and Kiowa raiders. A little scout work for the long knives who can't track a short buffalo in a deep snow. You?"

John wrapped an arm around the solid shoulders of his Tonkawa friend. "Raising calves and kids, Pete. How's the wife?"

Pete chuckled. "Ugly as ever. Temper like a scorpion. The Kiowa in her, I reckon. Wasn't her fault, so I don't hold it against her."

The two leaned against the wall of the general store and traded yarns for a few minutes. Whiskey Pete was on loan to the army garrison at Fort Griffin, but would be rejoining Colonel Ranald Mackenzie's force in a few weeks for a major campaign against the Comanche and Kiowa in the sprawling Staked Plains.

"This Mackenzie's a little touched by the sun," Pete said, "but he's one helluva fighter. Come along with us, John. Have some fun. You maybe work too hard. Huntin' Comanch'll put an edge back on you. Straighten your pecker better'n cheap whiskey."

John sighed. "Pete, I have a family to worry about now. Can't go chasing all over creation anymore. But, by God, I would if I could." He pushed himself away from the wall. "I'll go buy us a bottle." He glanced around the street. "Everybody else is drunk, looks like. We might as well join them."

Pete waved away the offer. "Not this Tonk, John. Don't drink. Never have."

"Then why do they call you Whiskey Pete?"

The Tonkawa shrugged. "Who knows? White man makes no more sense than an Indian most of the time. See you around, John Selman. Watch your hair."

"And you watch yours, Pete. My place is the Rock Ranch over on Tecumseh Creek. You're welcome there any time."

John Selman watched the Tonk walk away. *Good man,* he thought. *With Whiskey Pete and Ranald Mackenzie on the trail, old Quanah Parker and his bunch may not be long for this earth.*

The feeling he was being watched prickled the hairs of John's forearms. It was a danger sign that he had long ago learned to heed. He sensed a presence at his back and turned.

Three brawny buffalo hunters stood a few paces away. All three carried the big rifles that marked their trade. John recognized the big one in front. His name was Haulph. He was bad medicine when he had been drinking, and no one in The Flats could remember ever seeing the man sober. He had already beaten one man to death and carved up a second with a skinning knife. John did not know the other two.

Haulph stared at John, a sneer on the wide, scarred face that showed above a soiled beard. "Anything I can't stand," Haulph said, "it's a damn Injun-lover."

"Man has a right to his opinions, Haulph," John said, his voice calm. He sized up his situation and didn't like the fit of it. John knew he and the Henry could take the big man, but the other two complicated matters. Even if he downed two, the odds were he would collect a big chunk of lead before it was over. A buffalo gun at short range was bad medicine.

"What ya think, fellas? Wanna teach this Injun-lover a thing or two?" Behind Haulph, John saw the crowd begin to thin as people eased away from the possible line of fire.

John tensed his thumb on the hammer of the Henry, a slow anger gnawing at his gut. *It just might be worth the gamble.*

"Trouble, Mister Selman?"

The voice came from John's left, toward the edge of the street. John chanced a quick glance. A young man sat astride a compact sorrel horse, a new Winchester rifle resting across the horn of his saddle. The muzzle was pointed toward the stocky buffalo hunter on John's left.

The hunter glanced nervously from John to the rider. It was obvious to John that the buffalo shooter all at once didn't like the odds quite so much.

"Selman?" The second hunter's question carried a tinge of uncertainty.

"That's right," the rider said. "John Selman. It's always a good thing to know the name of the man who kills you."

The second man swallowed. "Selman, I didn't know it was you. I want no trouble with you." He lowered the muzzle of his buffalo gun and raised a hand.

John glared at Haulph. "Your friend seems to have his wits about him, mister." He kept his voice steady and calm with an effort. "Now, you and I have a small problem. I suppose how this works out depends on you."

The buffalo hunter's stained beard twitched. "Heard about you, Selman. Didn't hear nothin' scared me much." Haulph turned his head and spat.

John had the Henry cocked and shouldered, the muzzle pointed at the bridge of Haulph's nose, before the tobacco juice hit the ground. The buffalo hunter's eyes narrowed. John half smiled. "Your play, Haulph. Piss or get off the pot."

For a moment John thought the big buffalo hunter was going to make his move. Then Haulph lowered his rifle. "Aw, hell, Selman. We was just hoorawin' you a little."

John let the obvious lie slide. He kept the Henry trained on Haulph's head until the big man turned and walked away. John watched until he was sure the buffalo men intended no trickery, then lowered the hammer of the Henry and turned to the man on the sorrel.

"Much obliged," he said. "That could've got a little sticky."

The horseman dismounted in a fluid, easy motion. He was, John guessed, in his early twenties, with a slender build, lively blue eyes, a quick grin, and a scraggly goatee to go with a full mustache. The horseman extended a hand. "John Larn," he said. "Glad to meet you, Selman."

Larn's grip was strong, with a dry palm despite the tension of the last few minutes.

"I don't make it a habit of butting into other people's quarrels," Larn said, "but since we're going to be neighbors I figured I had a personal interest." Larn nodded in the direction of the departed buffalo hunters. "Don't like the looks of that big one. Maybe you should have just killed him."

"Wish now I had, Larn." John shouldered his rifle. "You say we're neighbors?"

"I bought some land just down the road a ways from your place." Larn waved toward a nearby saloon. "Buy you a drink?"

"I'll do the buying," John Selman said.

Edna Selman was impressed anew each time she entered the Camp Cooper ranch home designed and built by John Larn for his wife, Mary. Edna's own home was one of the finest in the territory, but it seemed drab compared to the Larns' near-palace of six rooms with a glassed-in cupola. Mary's touch was apparent throughout the place. The hardwood floors were clean and polished. Bright draperies, curtains, and lively paintings competed with Navajo wall hangings to brighten the rooms.

The Larn ranch was only two miles from the Selmans' place on the Clear Fork. The two men ran their herds together on the open range nearby, and seldom a week passed that the Larns and Selmans did not gather for a meal and an evening of socializing.

Edna sometimes wondered if the stories told about John Larn were true or just frontier campfire yarns. It was said he had killed several men, including a deputy sheriff, before his arrival in Fort Griffin. She didn't think it possible.

John Larn seemed anything but a killer. He was always courteous and kind to her. A quick, easy laugh lay just beneath the surface of the deep blue eyes that highlighted his thin but handsome face. And it was obvious that he was as devoted to Mary as she was to him. John Larn could be an eloquent speaker when the occasion demanded, and he didn't mind getting down in the dirt to play mumblety-peg with a child. His wife was a study in polish and charm, tall, slender, and gracious. It was little wonder they moved with ease in the upper social circles of wealthy ranchers and politicians. Yet they were just as much at ease with the working men and women of the rough-hewn and frequently dangerous country.

Still, Edna couldn't help but wonder. Even in his own home John Larn always wore a gun. It was something that didn't quite seem to fit.

She forced her mind away from its idle musings and sipped at the tea in the delicate porcelain cup. Mary was playing with the baby. She had become almost a second mother to the Selman children.

Today's visit was more than simply social. From time to time Mary excused herself and disappeared into the back room that served as her husband's office, carrying coffee and cigars. Bits of conversation and the aroma of tobacco smoke drifted from the room as Mary entered or left.

Among those in the back room were some of the area's most powerful men, ranchers and prominent merchants. Edna and Mary both knew the women also had a stake in the meeting. The region was violent and lawless. Hardly a family represented there had not been the victim of rustlers, thieves, or other scoundrels. Edna hoped the gathering of men could find a way to restore the peace.

J. D. McLochlin stood behind John Larn's desk in the crowded room. He took a sip from the brandy snifter in his right hand, savored the rich flavor, then lowered the drink.

"So, gentlemen," the rancher said, "something must be done. There will be no law in this area until the county is organized, and that is at least a year in the future." He paused for dramatic impact. "In the old days around Fort Davis, we enforced our own law. That enforcement committee no longer exists."

McLochlin sipped again at the brandy. "I propose, therefore, that a new vigilance committee be formed, headed by Mister John Larn and Mister John Selman. Each of us will participate or supply men and animals when needed. And, by God, we'll reclaim our land and our peace from the outlaws and thieves who would take it from us."

McLochlin listened to the muttered assent, the calls of "Here, Here!" and saw heads nod in agreement. He sighed in satisfaction. Selman and Larn were now allies, McLochlin men, even if they didn't know it. A man could manipulate allies. After the criminal element—to McLochlin, anyone who stood in his way—

was chased from the Clear Fork, the McLochlin organization could then turn its hand against the real threat on the horizon— the grangers, dirt farmers who crowded in, took over the free range, and put it to death beneath their cursed plows. Then, when the time was right, he would eliminate Selman and Larn. That would be no great problem. A herd of men were much easier to handle than a herd of surly Longhorn cattle. And a stocky little Scot would become the richest man in North Texas. Maybe in the entire state. Not bad, he thought, for the son of a poor tinsmith.

King James Peter Wolfpelt strolled down the dusty main street of The Flats toward the general store, fingering the coins in his pockets. They would buy enough chewing tobacco to last until Colonel Mackenzie sent word to him to report for scout duty with the Fourth Regiment.

The portly Tonkawa's face darkened as he spotted the buckskin gelding tied to the hitch-rail of the Red Dog Saloon across the street. The animal's flanks were deep hollows. Lather had dried in salt-crusted streaks on the horse's sides. Spur marks whelped the buckskin's shoulders and ribs. Its head drooped. The horse had obviously been without water for a long time, yet just around the corner of the saloon stood a full trough.

Whiskey Pete snorted in disgust. Only a white man would neglect an animal that way. Suffering in a Comanche, or even a real human being, Pete could tolerate. But not in a horse.

He crossed the street, untied the gelding, and started to lead it to water. At his back he heard the door of the saloon swing open.

"What the hell are you doing, Injun!"

Pete turned to face a big man, face flushed with whiskey and rage.

"The animal needs water," Pete said simply.

The big man's hand went to his belt. "I'll tend to my own damn horse, you red bastard!"

Whiskey Pete saw the flash from the muzzle of the gun and felt the heavy slam of the slug into his chest just before the world went black.

Haulph stood above the Tonkawa and emptied his pistol into the body.

• • • •

John Selman swung the barrel of his rifle toward the approaching rider, irritated that his hunt had been interrupted. The young whitetail deer would be a half mile away by now. It would be beans and dried beef for supper again tonight.

He lowered the hammer of the Henry and slid it back into its saddle boot as he recognized the horseman. He squatted on his heels and waited as the Tonkawa known as Lucas reined his rangy palomino to a stop before John. The Indian's hair was cropped short in a symbol of grief.

"John Selman, I am sorry to disturb you in the middle of your hunt," Lucas said. "It is something you should know. Your wife told me I might find you here."

"What is it, Lucas?"

"Your friend and mine. James Peter. He has been killed."

John felt the shock slam onto his belly like ice water. "How did it happen, Lucas?"

The Tonkawa dismounted and squatted next to John. "It was the man called Haulph. The mean one. A true son of a she-dog. He rode into Griffin two days ago. Left his horse at the hitch-rail a night and a day. Whiskey Pete came by. He saw the horse and was leading it to drink. Haulph came from the saloon, blind drunk. He saw Pete with the horse and shot him. Six times."

John felt the lump in his gut warm in the beginning of rage. *I should have shot that sonofabitch when I had the chance.*

"James Peter did not know of this Haulph. He did not know that no one else dared care for the horse for fear of Haulph. James Peter knew only that the horse was near death from thirst," Lucas concluded.

"Lucas, where is Haulph now?"

"The town marshal put him in jail." Lucas's face twisted in disgust. "It is said that when he recovers from the drink, he will be freed. It is no crime in The Flats to kill a Tonk."

John Selman's fingers traced the outline of the receiver on the Henry. "It's a crime to kill a friend of John Selman," he told the Tonk. "Lucas, I have a favor to ask. Tell my wife I have a job to do, that I may not be home for a couple of days. Ask her not to worry."

The Tonkawa nodded his understanding. John swung into the

saddle, then leaned down to grasp the Indian's hand. "Thank you for bringing me this sad news, Lucas. For being a friend. When this man Haulph is freed from jail, I'll be waiting."

John reined his horse toward The Flats. Lucas watched until the white man disappeared from view beyond a ridge. "Haulph will soon walk the long darkness," he said aloud, "and King James Peter Wolfpelt will find peace."

John Larn studied the face of the dead man in the wagon bed. Haulph's sightless eyes stared toward the coppery sun overhead. A lead slug had entered just above the bushy eyebrows in the center of the forehead. Larn did not need to turn the body to know what the back of the head looked like. He flipped the dirty blanket over the face and turned to the two men with him.

Even in a lawless town like The Flats, some formalities had to be followed. "Looks like a clear case of suicide to me," Larn said.

The two others nodded in agreement. "No great loss," one of them said, producing a stub of pencil. He scribbled for a moment in a tattered book, then handed the pencil to Larn, who added his name to the official inquest finding. The third man did the same. The finding was now a matter of record. None of the men had any quarrel with the verdict. The suicide ruling did, in a most logical way, fit the situation. None said so, but all knew that any man who abused or killed a friend of John Selman had done the same as put a gun to his own head.

"What do we do with Haulph now?" the man with the record book asked.

Larn shrugged. "Load him in my wagon. I'll bury him on the way home."

Four miles from town and well off the main roads, John Larn dragged the body from the back of the wagon and shoved it over the edge of a ravine. He glanced at the buzzards circling overhead. "Dinner time, fellows," he said.

Griffin, Texas
Spring 1875

John Selman thumbed up the corner of the hole card before him
on the felt poker table in the Drovers Camp Saloon on Worth
Street. King of clubs. The first up-card dropped around the table.
John caught a nine of hearts.

"Queen bets," John Larn said, rippling the deck with slender
fingers. Larn had to raise his voice to be heard over the growing
din of the Friday night crowd at the Drovers. The place was
packed. The town had outgrown its original nickname of The
Flats and was known now simply as Griffin to the cowboys who
followed the steady stream of Texas cattle up the Western Trail.

John Selman knew it would be standing room only in the Drovers an hour from now, and only a matter of time until the first
fight broke out. The mix of cowboys, farmers, soldiers, merchants, drifters, whores, and gamblers was a cocked and primed
pistol needing only a touch on the trigger to explode. An increas-
ing number of buffalo hunters—tough and dangerous men to
whom killing was an accepted way of life—added another charge
of powder to the potential explosion.

John accepted the buffalo hunters. The men with the big guns
were performing a service. John agreed with General William
Sherman's idea that annihilation of the buffalo would put a quick
and permanent end to the Indian troubles. And since Colonel
Ranald Mackenzie's Fourth Regiment had swept through the winter camp of the Comanche and Kiowa a few months ago, Indian
raids in the Griffin area had all but stopped. The hide wagons that
rumbled into and out of Griffin meant the end of the Plains tribes.

John would miss the buffalo, in a way, but the damn shaggies
did eat a lot of grass that could be better used raising cattle.

He forced his attention back to the game. Besides himself, four
players sat around his table at the moment; more would-be gamblers waited impatiently for someone to drop out and leave a
chair empty at one of the half-dozen poker tables.

Billy Bland had the high card, a spade queen. The young cowboy tossed a quarter onto the table. John Selman had liked Bland the first time they met. He was small, cat-quick, with an easy smile and a penchant for women, whiskey, and good times. He was also a top hand with a gun and a horse. Selman wasted little time in recruiting Billy Bland into the Vigilantes. Larn, Selman, and Bland had fallen into the easy habit of running together. Where one was seen, the other two wouldn't be far away.

Bill Cruger toyed with his cards for several seconds before calling the bet. The hesitation did not escape John Selman's notice. For a man who wanted to be sheriff of Shackleford County, it took Cruger an uncommon amount of time to make a decision. Rancher Jim Mattison snorted in disgust and folded his hand.

Joe Watson called, then wiped a kerchief across a sweat-specked brow. Watson had downed a couple too many and was feeling the impact of the Drovers' uncut whiskey. *He doesn't know the Vigilantes have his name on the list,* John mused, *and here he is donating his money to three of us.* Selman and Larn both called.

By the last round of betting, only Bland, Larn, and Selman remained in the chase for the pot that had grown in the center of the table. Selman had a pair of nines and the spade king up, club king in the hole. He tossed a dollar bill onto the felt.

"Too rich for my blood," Bland said, folding his cards.

Larn half grinned at Selman, then folded. "Your pot," he said. The two friends had an unspoken agreement not to buck each other head-on in any game, regardless of the stakes. Each had seen too many friendships dashed on the turn of a card.

Mattison watched as Selman pulled in the money. Then he pushed his chair back. "Cards aren't running for me tonight, boys." A merchant who had been waiting patiently took Mattison's seat.

A haze of tobacco smoke had fogged the upper third of the Drovers Camp two hours later as Larn stood and pocketed the coins and bills before him. "Enough for tonight." Larn's goatee twitched in a grin. "Selman, there's somebody here I want you to meet."

John Selman swept his own winnings from the table. He was up about fifty dollars for the night, he figured, almost two month's wages for a working cowhand.

Larn had elbowed his way to a spot at the bar and ordered whiskey for both of them. Larn tilted his glass toward a door leading to the back rooms of the saloon.

"There she is now." He waved a hand and caught the attention of a tall brunette clad in a low-cut gown, the skirt tucked up and under to mid-thigh. The woman smiled and waved back, then started to work her way through the crowd. Selman studied her as she approached. Long, shapely legs, round breasts, a nipped waist that seemed bound by no corset, and full hips that swayed an invitation as she moved. Her facial features were short of outright beauty, but attractive, accentuated by deep brown eyes flecked with gold on high cheekbones. She brushed off a pair of groping hands with a "Not now, sugar—maybe later," and gave Larn a greeting kiss on the cheek.

"God, John. It's been a long time. New Mexico, right?"

"It's been too long, Minnie," Larn said. His tone was soft, wistful. Then he grinned. "New Mexico. We did have some times. Owner of this particular Sodom told me you were coming in tonight. Minnie, I want you to meet a friend of mine. John Selman, Minnie."

John took the slender hand extended to him. Her long fingers were warm to the touch. "A pleasure to meet you, Minnie," he said.

"Selman, I'm going to do you a favor I would do no other man," Larn said. His grin was wider. "Since I'm a happily married man now and a respected member of Griffin society, I give you, John Selman, my share of this woman. She's expensive. But by God, she's worth it."

John Selman wondered if the heat in his cheeks was from the woman or the whiskey; he knew he was near his limit. He could tell John Larn had already passed the fork in his own liquor road.

"Mister Selman." Minnie canted her head to one side, studying John's face, a smile on her full lips. "I feel like I've just been traded like a Longhorn cow."

"Now, Minnie—"

"Don't you say anything, John Larn. I didn't say I wasn't pleased with the trade." Minnie slipped her hand beneath Selman's arm, glanced from one to the other, and then shook her head. "John Selman. John Larn. Too many Johns around here.

Last names are too formal for friends and too troublesome for business."

"Tell you what, Minnie," Larn said with a wink, "he's about sixty years older than I am. Why not call me John and him Gray-headed Old Bastard?"

John Selman chuckled and reached for his glass. "Why not call me John and this young saddle bum Selman's Other Brother. Just call him by the initials."

Minnie's laugh was husky and musical, climbing partway up the scale and sliding down again. John Selman liked the sound of it. She squeezed his arm. "If one of you gentlemen will buy me a drink, I'll solve this problem. You, sir," she pointed to Larn, "are now Young John. And you, Mister Selman, are Old John. No disrespect intended, of course."

Larn leered at Minnie. "You might want to call him Long John before the night's out, Minnie."

Selman flushed. He was about to reply when a hand dropped onto Minnie's bare shoulder.

"How much you charge, lady?"

John Selman's smile faded. He knew the voice. Hank Floyd. Drifter and running mate of Joe Watson. Like Watson, a member of the McBride gang of thieves and rustlers. Another of the names on the Vigilantes' list. Selman eased Minnie's hand away from his arm and turned to face the muscular Floyd. The man was about two hours past sober and a month beyond a bath.

"The lady is with me, Floyd," Selman said. "Take your hand off her."

Floyd wavered on his feet, trying to focus his gaze on Selman's face. "Hell you say," he mumbled. "Whores go to the man with the cash—" His words ended in a choked gasp. The muzzle of John Selman's Colt rammed against the underside of Floyd's jaw.

"I said she's with me, Floyd. Now, take your hand off. Or I take the top of your head off."

"Mister Selman, I can take care of—"

"Shut up, Minnie," Larn interrupted. "It's Hank's turn to call or fold. I'd kind of like to see how this turns out."

Hank Floyd's hand fell away from Minnie's shoulder. "Damn you, Selman, I'll—"

Selman pushed the gun muzzle deeper into the tender flesh.

Floyd raised himself on tiptoes and made a strangled sound. "You won't do a damn thing, Floyd. Except leave." Selman held the drifter that way for a few seconds, then lowered the gun. Floyd gasped for air, face twisted in hate.

"I won't forget this, Selman." The drifter's voice was a hoarse croak. "I'll nail your hide to a tree."

John Selman shrugged. "Any time you feel stud enough, Floyd, I won't be hard to find."

Hank Floyd tried one last baleful glare, then turned and walked unsteadily away. John Selman turned his back to the man and lifted his whiskey glass.

"Mister Selman, I appreciate your concern, but I do believe I know how to handle men on my own." Minnie's tone was aloof, with a sharp edge to it.

"Not that one, honey," John Larn said with a shake of the head. "He likes to hit women. Beat one to death down in Juarez, I hear. Old John here just did you a favor."

Minnie dropped her gaze, then slid her hand back under John Selman's arm. "I'm sorry. I didn't know. I shouldn't have scolded you, Mister Selman."

John felt the soft warmth of her breast against his arm, the firm pressure of her hip on his. "It's nothing. And I thought you were going to call me Old John."

"I always pay my debts, Old John." Minnie snuggled against him, her voice low. "I don't officially start work for another hour." She stared into Selman's face for a moment. "Old John, I want to know something. You turned your back on that man, and he was carrying a pistol. How did you know he wouldn't shoot you?"

Old John Selman grinned at her. "Because a gent named Young John was keeping an eye on him for me. He would have put six holes in Hank Floyd before Floyd could have turned around."

John Larn shrugged. "That's what friends are for." He leaned forward and kissed Minnie on the cheek. "God, Minnie. Times like this I wish I didn't have such a saint for a wife. Well, you two mere mortals have fun. Old John, I'll see you tomorrow. If you can still walk."

• • • •

Old John Selman and Young John Larn stood beneath the cotton-wood tree and watched the last bit of life twitch out of the two men caught with Jim Mattison's cattle. The altered brands were still fresh.

At Old John's side, Billy Bland sighed in satisfaction. "How many does that make, Old John? Ten in the last two weeks?"

"You should know, Billy. You tied the knots."

Billy Bland pulled a tobacco sack from his pocket and rolled a smoke. "Reckon I did at that. Special knot I learned from a real hangman. Sort of the Vigilante signature around here these days." He fired his cigarette and waved toward the two bodies. "Want to let 'em down, or just leave 'em hang?"

"Ease them down," John Larn said. "One of those ropes is mine, and good hemp's expensive." He glanced around the circle of riders, then grinned. "Damn shame that another bunch of rustlers got away again, isn't it, boys?"

Grim laughter rippled through the ranks of the riders. The "escape" of rustlers was a standing joke with members of the Shackleford County Vigilante Committee. That and "killed while trying to escape."

John Selman watched as the bodies were lowered. "Kind of like swimming upstream," he said to Larn. "Hang two, four more take their places. Hang four, eight more come in. You'd think word would have gotten around by now it's not a good idea to steal Shackleford County cattle."

"Some people take a lot of convincing." Larn coiled his rope. "We do our job well."

"Maybe too well," Selman said. "Seems like we're picking up enemies faster than friends. I overheard talk around Griffin that we're as bad as the people we hang."

"Depends on what side of the fence you're on, Old John." Larn swung into the saddle. "We got the strongest fence. We got the backing of McLochlin, Dewees and Bishop, Matthews, several other big brands. That makes us the biggest and meanest bull in the pasture."

Larn had a point, John thought. Most of the group's opposition didn't amount to much. A handful of dirt farmers, a few small-time ranchers, and a merchant or two weren't all that much of a threat.

Selman glanced around the group of vigilantes. Tough men, all good with guns, top horsemen. In addition to himself and Larn, this particular posse included Bill Cruger, W. H. Ledbetter, C. K. Stribling, and Jim Draper, all politically powerful men in the county. The names were supposed to be secret, but Old John suspected most of Griffin and Albany had a pretty good idea who did their dirty work for them.

Billy Bland waved toward the bodies beneath the tree. "Want to bury 'em, Young John?"

"Nah. Coyotes and buzzards will take care of it." Larn reined his horse to face the group. "Thanks, boys. If you'll kick these cattle back to Jim Mattison's place, I'll buy the drinks later in town. Old John, ride along with me. Got something we need to talk over."

Selman mounted. The two waited until the rest of the riders had the Mattison cattle lined out and were beyond earshot, then kneed their horses toward Griffin.

"John," Larn said, "McLochlin and some of the others put a bee in my hat the other day. They want to run me for sheriff come fall. They all but guaranteed me the votes."

"You'd be a good man for the job," Selman said.

Larn raised a hand. "There's more to it. The deal is, after I'm elected I appoint Bill Cruger first deputy. That's the hoss trading of politics. Cruger's a McLochlin man through and through. But I need a man I can trust to help me clean up this county, John. I can get you a constable appointment, maybe second deputy. No salary involved, but you'll make enough on fees to live well. Interested?"

John Selman didn't hesitate. "Hell, yes. I've always had an itch to be a lawman. Give me a good chance to scratch it and see if it feels good."

John Larn grinned. "Good. Not a man alive I'd rather have riding with me, you old badger." They rode in silence for a few minutes, then Larn turned once again to Selman. "First order of business after the election," he said, "is that we go after the McBride gang. That's going to take some good guns."

That was an understatement at best, John Selman told himself. Doc McBride's bunch had a dozen guns. McBride and his boys were behind most of the rustling that plagued the county. There was no easy way to take them in a daylight raid on their headquarters, a shack on the Clear Fork owned by Indian Kate and her daughter Swayback Mag, both whores of the first order. The Vigilantes would have to catch them in the open or pay a high price.

John Selman felt his pulse quicken. Breaking the McBride gang might kill an extra snake, too. If he were lucky, he might get Hank Floyd and Joe Watson in his gunsights. The two had been making talk ever since the night in the Drovers Camp, and John Selman was tired of watching his back.

"Be a tough hide to chew on, Young John," he said.

"You, me, Tom and Billy, and a few others I have in mind could do the job." Larn's easy confidence showed in his voice. "All we got to do is find the right time."

"Just holler when you're ready," Selman said.

Griffin, Texas
Winter 1875

Bill Cruger shifted in his seat in front of J. D. McLochlin's desk and waited as the Scot puffed his customary cloud of pipe smoke and squinted through the haze.

"Bill, I hope you understand why I'm going about this election the way I am. I know you want the job as sheriff. Bear with me a while and you'll have it."

Cruger nodded grudgingly. "I trust your judgment, Mister McLochlin."

"Good. Now, we both know Larn has this election tied up like a dogie calf. He has a lot of friends and just about as many enemies. His friends will vote for him out of loyalty and his enemies will vote for him hoping he'll get killed. Even without my influence—and that of the other big stockmen—he'd probably be the next sheriff, anyway. At any rate, he'll take you on as chief deputy. When Larn and his friend Selman have served their purpose, we eliminate them. Then the badge is yours."

McLochlin paused, fumbled for a fresh match, and fired the pipe again. "Until then, I want you on the inside. I want to know when Larn and Selman take a piss, where, and what color it is. I'll more than make up the difference in salary between sheriff and first deputy. You'll not be troubled for money."

Bill Cruger fished the makings from a shirt pocket, rolled a cigarette, and did his part to thicken the smoke as he analyzed his own position. He didn't have the political base to carry a county-wide election. Even if he thought he might have a chance to win, he wouldn't risk going up against Larn. Several men had tried it over one thing or another. All they got for their efforts was a chunk of lead or a short drop from a tree limb. There was no reason to believe Larn would look any more kindly on a political challenge than he would a personal insult. The sheriff's job was a prize, but it wasn't worth dying over. Not when a man could just wait it out.

Cruger snuffed his cigarette in an over-full ash tray. "How do you propose to get Larn and Selman out of the way, Mister McLochlin?"

The rancher half smiled. "I've my own methods, Bill. I'll let you in on it when the time is right." McLochlin stood, the signal that the meeting was over.

"All right, Mister McLochlin. As I said, I trust your judgment."

The rancher reached across the desk and extended a hand. "Excellent, Bill. Just keep your powder dry for now. Between us, we'll tame Shackleford County. On our own terms."

J. D. McLochlin watched from a smudged window as Bill Cruger mounted and rode away toward Griffin. *All it takes to own a county,* he told himself with a smile, *is to own the sheriff and the county judge. And Bill Cruger will be a hell of a lot easier to control than Larn and Selman.*

Griffin, Texas
Spring 1876

Edna Selman spooned the last of the redeye gravy over young William's second helping of ham and biscuits, then stared for a moment at her own untouched breakfast. The fried egg glared back at her, a yellow eye floating in ham grease. She knew she should force herself to eat; caring for four children and keeping a house took a lot of energy. Especially since the fourth, John Selman Jr., was still an infant. But the appetite just wasn't there.

Edna could not explain the hollow feeling that rose with her most mornings. On the surface, she had everything a woman could want. The kids were healthy, there was plenty of money, and she had a fine house and good friends. John seemed genuinely happy and at ease for the first time in months, maybe even years. Their lovemaking was more intense than ever, at least on the nights when John was home. John had been a constable since Larn's election as sheriff. His duties kept him away from the ranch two or three nights a week. But, she reasoned, it shouldn't be loneliness that caused the shuddery feeling that came over her on occasion. John had been gone from home many times in the past, often for days or weeks at a stretch, chasing Indians or outlaws. The overnight stays in Griffin shouldn't be cause for worry.

But they were.

Griffin was a violent town, one that never seemed to sleep. Sometimes at night when John was gone, Edna would awaken to the sound of gunfire ringing in her ears, a silent scream caught in her throat. The dream was infrequent but always the same. It had come again this morning, in the deep quiet before dawn.

Grandmother deGraffenreid was said to have "the gift," an ability to sense what was to come. Edna prayed that she had not inherited that gift.

"Sis? Are you all right?"

Tom's question jarred Edna from her inner world. She forced a smile. "I'm fine, Tom. Just thinking."

Hoofbeats sounded on the packed hardpan outside the ranch home. Tom was on his feet in an instant, handgun drawn and cocked. He was at the window in two strides. Edna watched him peer through the curtains, then relax.

"It's Jesse," Tom said.

Edna felt a frown crease her forehead. She didn't know how to take Jesse Evans. He was always pleasant to her, friendly with the kids. Edna knew that Jesse, John, and Tom had become close. But there was something about Jesse Evans. A hint of violence behind the gray eyes, a nagging sense that the man would kill at the slightest provocation. Or even for amusement.

She stood as Evans entered the room. "Morning, Jesse," Edna said. "Have a seat. I'll get some coffee. Have you had breakfast?"

Evans swept his hat from his head. "Thanks for the offer, Missus Selman, but I won't have time. I've come for Tom." Evans turned to Tom. "Better fetch your rifle and extra ammunition, Tom. The committee needs all hands in the saddle today."

Tom already had turned to the gun rack and the ammunition drawer beside it. "What's up, Jesse?"

"McBride's bunch. They finally made a mistake. Hit Ellison's place at dawn, stole twenty-six head of horses. Ellison saw them." Evans grinned. "Sheriff Larn's been waiting for this. We've got warrants. Larn and your brother have already cut their tracks. We'll clean that bunch out once and for all."

The echoes of the dream tumbled through Edna's mind. On impulse she grabbed Tom's arm. "Watch out, Tom. And tell John to be careful."

Tom casually patted Edna's hand. "Nothing to worry about, Sis. We're always careful."

John Selman knelt on the sandy north bank of the Brazos River and checked the loads in his Colt. The wagon tracks they followed were less than a quarter hour old.

He turned to the riders waiting just behind him. Tom Selman, Bill Cruger, the McLochlin rider named Everett, Billy Bland, Jim Draper, and G. R. Carter. He had ridden with them many times on Vigilante business, and trusted them all. Except Everett, maybe. There was something about the man, the way his eyes shifted all the time. But John knew Everett would hold up his end when the dance started. They would be more than a match for the rustlers up ahead.

The trail hadn't been easy; the McBride bunch weren't amateurs. And when they sensed the pursuit closing in, they had abandoned the stolen horse herd and split up. Three riders had turned north, toward the Dodge City Trail. John Larn, Jesse Evans and a couple more committee riders had taken off after them. Old John and his group stuck with the tracks of the rest of the gang.

"Tie down your war bonnets, boys," John said. "We'll be on them like a rooster on a grasshopper in a half hour." He mounted the sorrel and, with Tom at his side, nudged the gelding into a long lope.

Tom was the first to spot the fleeing rustlers. Four mounted men and a wagon, a half mile away. "There's two women with them. In the wagon."

John Selman muttered a quiet oath. "All right, fellows. Let's go get 'em. Don't shoot the women unless they shoot first." He waved his riders into a skirmish line.

The mounted rustlers bolted, leaving the slower wagon, as the Vigilantes closed ground. The wagon jolted over an unseen rock. The off rear wheel shattered and the wagon jolted to a stop. The two women, Sally Watson and a prostitute John had seen around Fort Griffin, jumped from the wrecked vehicle, hands raised.

"Leave them be for now," John yelled, "they aren't going anywhere." He spurred his sorrel toward the brush thicket where Joe Watson's horse had disappeared.

Thirty yards from the thicket, John heard a crack as a rifle slug ripped past his ear. He slapped a pistol shot toward the smoke. At John's left, Tom fired twice. John glanced toward his brother, saw Tom's horse seem to bunch up in mid-stride, then stumble. Tom kicked free of the stirrups. When the horse went down he landed on his feet, running, and fired again. John heard a yelp of pain from the thicket. At almost the same instant, a volley of shots sounded to the west.

John pulled his horse to a stop and dismounted, handgun at the ready. Ten feet away stood Joe Watson, pistol at his feet. Blood flowed from his right shoulder.

"You all right, Tom?" John called.

"Yeah. I think I nailed him with one."

John tossed a rope over Watson's chest, ignored the groan of pain, and led the wounded man toward the disabled wagon. Tom retrieved Watson's ground-hitched horse, switched the tack from his dead mount, and caught up with John.

"What do we do now, John?" he asked.

John listened to the distant gunfire. "We find a good tree. And wait."

An hour later the posse had once again formed up. Watson, a

man called Larapie Dan, and a rider known only as Reddy were in custody. All were wounded, Reddy the worst with a bullet hole in his rib cage. None of the committee riders had been hit.

John nodded toward Carter. "G.R., cut the wagon horses loose. Put the women on them and take them back to town." Carter reached for the knife at his belt. John knew the man had little taste for hangings and wouldn't mind the escort detail.

"What are you going to do with my husband, you sonofabitch?" Sally Watson's voice was shrill in the mild April air.

Selman turned an icy glare on the woman. "He'll likely wind up in jail. Which is where you're headed, too, if you don't shut up."

Sally Watson cursed steadily and fluently until Carter physically picked her up and deposited her on the harness horse. The other woman mounted silently on her own.

"Watch out for them, G.R.," John warned. "I wouldn't trust either of them as far as I can throw that wagon. The squaws are always the most vicious."

John and the remaining committee members waited until Carter and the women were out of sight. John turned to Watson.

"Where's McBride?"

"Reckon he got away, Selman," Watson said through teeth gritted in pain.

"I got a slug into his horse," Bill Cruger said. "He won't be hard to find."

Ten minutes later, the Vigilante riders sat and smoked under a red oak tree. Three bodies swayed in the light breeze at the end of ropes tossed over a stout limb.

"Hey, fellows," Billy Bland said, "you should have seen the way young Tom here come off his horse when it got shot out from under him. Landed on his feet and come up shootin', he did. Landed on his feet just like a cat."

One of the other riders chuckled. "Tom the Cat. Sounds like a good moniker to me. Tom Cat Selman."

John glanced at Tom. The youth's cheeks colored slightly, but there was a smile on his face. From that point on, John knew, Tom Selman would be saddled with a nickname for the rest of his life. Tom Cat.

John knocked the ashes from his pipe and stood. "Somebody

let these rustler carcasses down. We still have to find old Doc McBride."

The search lasted two hours before the footsore McBride was boosted onto Bland's horse in the shade of a pecan tree, a noose around his neck. Bland led the horse from under McBride.

John Selman sat astride his sorrel gelding, his gaze sweeping the northern horizon. "Wonder how Young John's making out? Bet my dollar on Larn. Hank Floyd and Bill Henderson might as well put a gun in their mouths and pull the trigger. Wish I was there to help." He sighed. "Anybody got a pencil and paper?"

Bill Cruger produced a stub of a pencil and a blank page from the small notebook he carried.

John printed the words with care:

> He said his name
> was McBride, but
> he was a liar as
> well as a thief

John kneed his skittish horse up to McBride's body and pinned the note to the dead rustler's shirt with a thorn.

"Leave him hang, boys," he said. "Let's go home. I believe we've earned us a drink."

FOUR

Griffin, Texas
Fall 1876

John Selman slouched in his customary seat at the corner poker table in the Drovers Camp Saloon. The place was quiet now. The herd-trailing season had passed, and most of the buffalo hunters were out on the plains shooting shaggies. The serious drinkers were still nursing last night's mistakes, John speculated. It would be a few more hours until the morning dog stopped barking and the night wolf geared up to howl. The buzz of flies in the warm afternoon air was almost as loud as the lazy conversation in the saloon.

The stakes were hardly worth the effort of shuffling the deck, but were enough to pass the time. Billy Bland was having a run of good cards and grumbling that this never seemed to happen unless he were playing with friends for nickels and dimes. Jesse Evans's luck was running just the opposite.

"Ain't there any face cards in this damn deck?" Evans grumbled. "Where's all the gamblers, anyway?"

John Larn shrugged. "Early yet, Jesse. Keep your britches buttoned." Selman could tell from Larn's tone that the boredom was beginning to take its toll on the younger man as well. And, Selman knew, it was more than just lack of action that bothered Larn. Someone or something was driving a wedge through the tight ranks of the Vigilantes.

The talk had started just after the McBride incident. It intensified after Larn returned from Kansas with the two other McBride thieves in custody, Bill Henderson and Hank Floyd. The two had been taken from the Griffin jail by masked men and lynched within days.

Nobody mourned the McBride gang, at least no one who counted. But now the grangers were under siege. Shots fired into their homes. A farmer going off to plow and never coming home. Bodies floating in the Clear Fork. And always the whispers pointed to the vigilante group led by the two Johns.

Rumors persisted that the Larn and Selman herds were growing faster than nature permitted. Rustling charges—even just rumors—were bad medicine in this country.

John took the deck from Larn, turning the problem again in his mind. He kept coming up with a pair of names.

McLochlin and Cruger.

They seemed to be the only ones who would benefit from a breakup of the Vigilantes. Cruger wasn't smart enough to manipulate public opinion. He *was* smart enough not to go spreading rumors.

That left McLochlin.

John had noticed that every time night riders hit a homesteader or a farmer turned up dead, McLochlin wound up with the land claim. Sometimes he bought it for a pittance. More often a McLochlin rider would file a new claim on the place, put up a picket shack and a crude corral to meet the improvements requirement, and then ride back to the ML Ranch headquarters. As a result, McLochlin now owned a good chunk of Shackleford County.

John kept coming back to the idea that McLochlin's support of John Larn for sheriff had motives other than just stopping the cattle thefts. He wasn't at all convinced that McLochlin was as pure as Clear Fork springwater.

Selman had started to deal the cards when a stable hand hurried into the saloon, glanced around, and approached the table.

"Sheriff Larn, Shorty Collins just rode in," the swamper said. "You said you wanted to know if I seen him."

Larn slipped a silver dollar from a shirt pocket and tossed it to the swamper. "Thanks, Eldon." Larn slipped his forty-five from its holster, checked the loads, and spun the cylinder. "Got a warrant for Collins. Me and every other lawman from El Paso to Canada."

Jesse Evans emitted a low whistle. "Shorty Collins, huh? Young

John, that Collins is pure snake with a handgun. Reckon you need some help?"

"Nah. Old John and I can handle it. You two keep our chairs warm." Larn grinned. "Hell, there might be a real gambler come along. I'd hate to see my friends sheared like a Mexican sheep." Larn pushed back his chair and stood. "Ready, Old John?"

Selman slipped the thong from the hammer of his new Colt Peacemaker and jigged the weapon in its holster a couple of times. "Sheriff, let's go serve a warrant."

The two men stepped into the dusty main street of Griffin, blinking their eyes into focus in the afternoon sun. They had gone two blocks when Selman spotted a figure moving across the street toward the Beehive Saloon a few yards ahead. "There he is."

John Larn picked up the pace, Selman matching him stride for stride at his left hand. They were within twenty feet when Larn yelled, "Throw up your hands, Collins!"

Collins cursed and spun toward the lawmen, his hand jumping toward his waistband. John Larn's own weapon was barely half clear of its holster when the blast of Selman's handgun jarred his ears. Collins staggered a step back at the impact of the first slug. Selman thumbed the hammer of the Colt three more times. Dust and fragments of cloth kicked from Collins's shirt pocket at the impact of each chunk of lead. The gunman spun and fell.

"Jesus," Larn said. "I didn't even have time to clear leather. Knew you were fast with a handgun, but that's ridiculous!"

John Selman half smiled. "Cheated. Pulled the gun before you hollered." He tilted the muzzle of the gun up, worked the ejection rod to kick the spent cartridges from the chamber, and thumbed fresh loads into the weapon. "Fast don't count as long as you're first. Bet you a dollar you can cover the four holes in Collins's chest with the ace of spades."

"Call."

The bet was no contest. Larn flipped a silver dollar to Selman, who plucked it from the air. "Seed money," he said. "I feel a string of good cards coming on."

"Save my chair. Soon's I get the formalities cleaned up on our friend here, I'll be in to win my dollar back."

The streets of Griffin were already buzzing with news of the gunfight by the time John Selman resumed his seat at the poker table. He felt the curious glances tossed his way from the growing crowd inside the Drovers Camp. Selman ordered a whiskey and reached for the cards.

"This an open game or a private matter?"

Selman looked up. A tall, broad-shouldered man, with a heavy handlebar mustache and a Colt holstered high on a slender waist, stood beside the table.

"Open game," John said. "We were hoping for some new blood."

"Got room for another one too?"

"Sure, why not."

The tall man waved toward the bar. A thin man with a chalky complexion strode toward the table, shoulders hunched as if in pain beneath a starched shirt and silk suit.

"I'm Wyatt Earp," the tall man said. "This is a friend of mine. Doc Holliday."

John rose, extended a hand. "John Selman. Heard of you, Earp. You too, Holliday." He made introductions around the table. "Pull up a chair. Game's five-card stud or jacks or better, dealer's pick. Two-bit ante, pot limit. Sheriff Larn'll be with us in a while. Cut for the deal?"

Holliday won the cut and dealt the cards, his fingers as nimble as his breathing was shallow and labored.

"Saw that action on the street," Earp said casually. "Pretty good shooting, Selman."

"New gun. Colt Single Action Army forty-five, six-and-a-half-inch barrel. Can't beat it for accurate."

"Walnut grips, I noticed," Earp said. "Prefer gutta percha myself. Hands sweat some. King bets four bits."

Two hands later John Selman knew he was in some heavy company when it came to poker. The stakes were already headed up, and John couldn't read these two the way he could the locals.

John Larn stomped into the saloon and sat heavily in the chair at Selman's right. "Dammit, Old John," he grumbled, "there's already talk out there that you gunned down an unarmed man. Rumors that Collins wasn't packing."

Selman snorted in disgust. "If that wasn't a Remington forty-four in his belt, I'll eat your best horse."

Earp nodded. "Shorty Collins was never more than arm's length from a gun since his mother slapped him off the tit. Wouldn't worry about it."

Larn seemed to notice the two new faces at the table for the first time. John made the introductions.

"I'll be damned," Larn said. "Wyatt Earp and Doc Holliday. Never thought I'd see the day I'd be cutting a deck with you two." Within minutes Larn seemed to have forgotten the fight with Collins.

John Selman folded his hand. A jack of hearts up and the spade five down didn't hold much promise. He glanced around the table. *Earp, Holliday, Larn, Selman, Evans, and Bland,* he thought. *One thing's for damn sure; nobody in his right mind would try to rob this poker game.*

The stakes gradually escalated until Billy Bland and Jesse Evans dropped out. "You fellows are out of my class with the cardboards," Bland said with a grin. "Come on, Jesse. Let's check out the Beehive while we can still afford a drink or two."

Two others were quick to take the seats vacated by Bland and Evans. Selman could tell by the expressions on their faces that they weren't as much interested in playing poker as they were in the chance to tell their kids and grandkids one day that they had played cards with Wyatt Earp and Doc Holliday. The crowd around the table grew as word spread that four gunfighters were playing at the same table. Most of them were probably wondering when the trouble would start.

It never did. Selman found Earp and Holliday to be pleasant company as well as top-shelf poker players. Holliday seldom spoke, but Earp was an easy talker.

"Sheriff Larn, did you ever run across a kid by the name of John Wesley Hardin?" Earp asked casually.

Larn nodded. "Wes Hardin. Yeah, I remember. He left his calling card nailed to the back bar at the Beehive. Three of spades with the center spade shot out. Three holes cloverleafed, another just a hair off. That was about three years ago, I guess. Just before he killed Deputy Webb over in Comanche. Friend of yours?"

Earp tossed a silver dollar into the pot, calling John Selman's bet. "Not exactly. Thought you might want to know young Wes stepped in it when he shot Webb. Got a Texas Ranger after him now. Man called John B. Armstrong."

"Call and raise a dollar," Larn said. Coins clinked on the table. "Hardin really kill thirty men, or is that just talk?"

Earp shrugged. "I wouldn't be surprised. Nasty bastard. Shoots people just for the hell of it." He sighed. "Guess I shouldn't be too hard on him. His kind keep lawmen like you and me in business."

"Yeah," Larn said with a wry grin, "for as long as we last."

The game broke up shortly after midnight. Larn was up about twenty dollars, and Selman had just about broken even. Earp and the consumptive Holliday had pocketed over a hundred from the other players who came and went.

Earp stood and offered a hand. "You gents get over Tombstone way, look us up. Hard to find good poker players who don't try to cheat these days."

"We'll do that, Wyatt," Larn said. "Watch your backside."

Larn sat back down and sipped at a whiskey until the Drovers Camp doors closed behind Earp and Holliday. "Old John," he said, contented, "I'd hate like hell to have to face either of those fellows over a gunsight."

John Selman merely nodded. There wasn't much to say.

Griffin, Texas
January 1877

John Selman sat at the workbench in a back room of his Rock Ranch home, lacing a new latigo to the D-shaped rigging ring of his brush-scarred saddle, and tried once again to figure out what the hell the people of Griffin expected of its lawmen. And of the Vigilantes. It didn't make sense.

Shackleford County was as near to being tamed as it ever had been. Cattle rustling, horse thievery, and robbery were beginning to lose their appeal, speeded along by reports such as the clipping he carried in his wallet. The paragraph from the *Austin Weekly Statesman* declared:

> No wonder the highwaymen are seeking
> security east of the Colorado. Eleven
> men were hanged ten days ago at Fort
> Griffin and four more are enroute to
> that merciful village. . . .

The clipping was dated December 28, 1876.

Still, the grumblings had intensified. Criticism of the Vigilante tactics grew every day, despite widespread acknowledgement that they worked.

The rangers had been called in, but so far they had been unable to find evidence linking the Vigilantes to any shootings, hangings, or the frequent raids on the granger homes.

Even the governor had pitched his chip into the pot. According to the *Statesman,* he had said that "when a jail is forced and prisoners taken out and murdered . . . the Sheriff and jailors are accessories to the crime . . . No Sheriff should be permitted to hold office another day after his jail has been forced . . ."

That, Selman knew, was a direct shot at John Larn. And by association, at himself.

John still couldn't figure the public wail over the shooting of Shorty Collins. No man had ever deserved being killed more. But the rumors still circulated that Collins wasn't carrying a weapon, that Selman was drunk and had shot down an unarmed man in cold blood.

Even more bothersome were the rumors that the Selman and Larn herds were expanding fast through rustled stock. No one in Griffin had the guts to say it to Selman's or Larn's face, but it got back to them.

John couldn't deny he might have taken a few liberties with the lariat. But what the hell. A slick was a slick, even if it was a yearling tagging after a cow with someone else's brand. The Clear Fork country was still mostly open range, and a rancher who didn't brand his own stock couldn't complain about a few head. John had taken no more than he felt justified in taking. A man was entitled to some compensation for the time he lost chasing rustlers and horse thieves. *If Larn and I had stolen half the cattle and done half the killing we're supposed to have,* John groused to himself, *both of us would be out of ammunition and butt-deep in livestock.*

John and Larn hadn't been able to pin down the source of the rumors, but there were indications that they came from within the vigilante group itself.

John pulled the damp rawhide laces tight, tied them off with a flat crossbuck knot, and pounded the knot flat with a small wooden mallet. When they dried, the lacings would be stronger than the latigo itself. He gave the leather strap two sharp tugs to make sure it was settled into the right position around the rigging ring.

John Selman could take the heat of public scorn and even the rumors of rustling. But he was worried about their effect on Edna. She seemed thinner, her skin paler. Her shoulders had begun to slump, and she didn't laugh as often these days. John made up his mind. He would find out, once and for all, who was spreading the stories. When somebody tried to hurt him, that was one thing. When somebody started to hurt his family, that was another.

He started at the light tap on the door, then silently cursed himself for being so jumpy. Edna opened the door to the workroom. "John, Jesse's here. There's been trouble in town. Billy Bland was killed last night."

John sat for a moment, stunned. "What—how?"

Jesse Evans stepped into the room. His hat was in his hand and John could see pain in the gunman's eyes.

"Cruger shot him, John." Jesse's voice was tight with anger.

"What happened?"

"Billy got a little liquored up. Him and Charlie Reed started a shooting contest. Blasting out the lights in the saloon. Cruger and William Jeffries went to break it up. Walked in with their guns drawn. Billy turned around, saw the gun in Cruger's hand, and touched one off. Creased Cruger's arm. Cruger shot back and all hell broke loose, everybody shooting. When it was over Billy was dead."

John spat a curse and slammed the mallet into the workbench top.

"Two other fellows in the Beehive got killed," Evans said. "A soldier and a lawyer. Jeffries took a slug in the chest and may, may not, make it. Reed got away."

John slumped at the workbench, the emptiness heavy in his

gut. After a moment he rose. "Edna, tell Tom Cat to saddle my sorrel." He turn to Jesse. "Larn know?"

Evans shook his head. "Rode on past the Larn place. I thought I'd better tell you first, John. God knows what Larn's going to do when he finds out. Figured it would take us both to keep him from killing Cruger on the spot."

John nodded. "You may be right." He led the way into the main room of the ranch house, lifted his rifle from the gun rack, strapped on his pistol belt, and strode outside to where Tom was tightening the cinch on the sorrel.

Edna and Tom watched as the two men, hunched in the saddle against the bite of the January wind, rode toward the Larn ranch. "Tom," she said to the man at her side, "is this ever going to end? All the killing? When is John going to ride off like this and not come back?"

Tom Selman draped a protective arm across Edna's shoulders. "Try not to worry, Sis," he said. "John Selman's no fool. He'll know what to do. Everything will be all right."

John Larn slammed a fist into the scarred walnut top of the desk in the sheriff's office and glared into Bill Cruger's face.

"Damn you to hell, Cruger!" Larn's voice strained under the weight of raw fury. "I ought to kill you where you sit."

Cruger shifted his weight nervously. "I didn't have a choice, Larn. Bland shot at me. Tried to kill me."

"Why the hell wouldn't he? You walk in there with a cocked pistol pointed at somebody, they won't stop to pass the time of day. Of all the stupid damn stunts you've ever pulled, Cruger, this one takes the prime cut!"

John Selman clamped a hand on Larn's forearm. "Don't make it worse, Larn," he said, and turned to glare at the deputy. "Cruger, you broke the biggest rule in the Vigilante code. You killed one of our own."

"I tell you, Selman, I didn't have a choice—"

"You had a choice, Cruger," John snapped. "It doesn't take a stud hoss gunfighter to stop a couple cowboys from celebrating a little. No need to go in with a gun in your hand. It's just too damn bad Billy's aim was off." He turned away from the deputy with a tug at Larn's arm. "Come on, Young John. Let's get out of here before one of us decides to kill this bastard."

Word of the Beehive gunfight and the confrontation between Selman, Larn, and Cruger wasn't long in reaching J. D. McLochlin.

The Scot stood at a window, listened to the moan of the wind against the pane, and smiled. In a few minutes in the Beehive, Bill Cruger had done on his own what might have taken months otherwise. It had been a dumb and unplanned move on Cruger's part. McLochlin wished he had thought of it.

The Vigilantes were now completely split into two distinct factions. Larn, Selman, and a handful of their friends on one side. Cruger and McLochlin allies on the other. The latter had the strength in numbers and political power.

McLochlin strode to the cluttered desk at the center of the room. It was time to call in a couple more favors. He reached for a pen and paper. He wrote for a few minutes, then stuffed, sealed, and addressed two envelopes. The last bit of bait for the trap. For two wolves.

Griffin, Texas
Spring 1877

John Selman drew a razor-edged butcher knife around the hock joint of the beef carcass, which lay on the bloodied table in the slaughter shed behind John Larn's ranch house. He levered the lower portion of the steer's leg against the edge of the table and pushed down. The joint parted with a sharp pop.

Selman tossed the bony lower leg into a scrap pile nearby and wiped beads of sweat from his forehead. Butchering beeves was awkward and hard work unless a man knew exactly what he was doing. Selman was an expert. He had learned the trade in the early days from his brother-in-law, Jasper deGraffenreid, who was a superb butcher.

John paused to wipe the blood from his hands and dip a drink of water from the nearby pail. This was the first beef of the day. Larn was off now looking for a second.

The government contract had come as a surprise to Old John. Selman and Larn had been chosen to supply beef for the soldiers at Fort Griffin and the Tonkawa settlement outside the fort. In addition, the two men had been appointed hide and animal inspectors for the herds of cattle moving up the busy cattle trail through Griffin.

The inspector's post was especially lucrative. The established fee for a herd inspection ranged from twenty to thirty dollars. Selman charged drovers twice that; sometimes more if he found stock in the herds that didn't belong there. The trail bosses were more than happy to kick in a bonus if the inspector failed to officially notice the brands not accounted for on the tally books.

Selman hadn't been at all surprised when Larn had abruptly resigned as sheriff of Shackleford County. He *was* surprised that Larn hadn't killed Bill Cruger, who now carried Larn's badge.

For many nights they had shared a bottle or two in Larn's home, planning the best way to get revenge on Cruger for killing Bland. Nothing came of their plans except ringing hangovers.

The beef contracts and herd inspections kept them too busy making money now to worry much about Cruger. Still, something didn't feel quite right about the whole setup. They hadn't asked for the contracts; the army and the chief state inspector of hides and animals had come to them. John Selman doubted it was their sterling reputations for honesty that attracted the deals.

Their new roles didn't stop the rumors. If anything, that situation was worse now. Enemies, like friends, didn't often go away. John tried to ignore the stories. He also never went anywhere without his rifle in hand, the Colt in his belt, and an eye peeled for anything that halfway spelled trouble.

He finished off the water and picked up his butcher knife.

A short time later he carried the steer hide to the edge of the deep hole on the Clear Fork behind Larn's ranch, weighted it down by wrapping the hide around a stone, and tossed it into the water. Traces of blood and wisps of pale tallow floated for a moment, then wandered away on the current as the hide sank.

Larn rode in a half hour later, hazing two fat long yearling steers into the holding pens behind the slaughter shed. Selman picked up the little top-break Smith & Wesson twenty-two and checked the chambers. The little gun was sufficient to kill beeves with a well-placed shot in the forehead, and cheaper and quieter to use than the big Colt.

Selman cocked the pistol and waited for the larger of the two steers to turn and face him.

"Company coming," Larn said quietly.

Selman lowered the handgun and turned to look. Thirteen men rode toward the ranch. John recognized most of them. Nine were Cruger men, Vigilantes. Cruger wasn't among them. Two of the other riders he had played poker with in the past; he remembered the faces, if not the names. Newton Jones, recruited into the Texas Ranger ranks from Griffin, rode alongside the leader, G. W. Campbell, Lieutenant, Texas Rangers. A bad man to tangle with.

Larn and Selman strode to the front of the house and waited patiently until Campbell and his contingent reined in before them.

"Mister Larn," the ranger said without the formality of a greeting, "I have a warrant to search the premises, particularly the area of the Clear Fork which runs by your place."

"And what," Larn challenged, "does that warrant give you the right to look for?"

Campbell held Larn's glare for several heartbeats. If there was any fear in the ranger, it didn't show. Selman figured the man's expression would be the same even if he were alone, without a dozen guns to back him. "The hides of beeves slaughtered here," Campbell said. "We have reason to believe some of them may be from stolen cattle."

For a moment, Selman thought Larn might swing his rifle toward the ranger. Then Larn shrugged. "I won't stand in your way." He started to hand his Winchester to the ranger. Campbell shook his head. "I only came to see the search carried out. If you don't refuse, I don't need to take your weapons."

"Then go ahead," Larn said. "You won't find anything."

"If I do," Campbell said, "I'll have to get a warrant for your arrest, Larn—and you, Selman."

"You do that, Lieutenant. But come back alone or with other

rangers. I'll go peaceably with you, but not with this clutch of snakes you're riding with.''

A week later John Larn and John Selman stood outside the Shackleford County courthouse. The charges had been dismissed. Campbell's party had found six branded hides that Larn couldn't account for in the Clear Fork, but the only man with nerve enough to testify had suddenly had a change of heart and was stricken by a need to see some new country.

Larn was in a jovial mood. "Well, Old John. Since we're in town anyway, let's have a drink and find a poker game. Been a while since I sliced a deck with anyone outside my own ranch house.''

Selman rolled a cigar across his mouth. Larn's mood was contagious, to a point. "Young John, I'll lift a glass and turn a card with you tonight. Maybe see if Minnie's available. But I've got a feeling we haven't heard the last of those hides just yet." He fired the cigar and exhaled a cloud of smoke. "Let's go tree a town. Real quiet-like.''

From his post across the street, J. D. McLochlin watched the two longtime friends start off in the direction of the Drovers Camp.

"Sorry, Mister McLochlin," Sheriff Bill Cruger said at the rancher's side. "I thought we had them nailed to the wall this time.''

McLochlin chuckled. "We did nail them, Bill. Maybe they didn't go to trial, but we got what we needed. Those two will be wearing the Clear Fork hides around their necks for a long time as far as most folks around here are concerned. All it takes now is timing and patience. They'll make a mistake.''

Cruger cleared his throat nervously. "I heard Old John tell Lieutenant Campbell those hides must have been put there by someone else to frame him and Larn. Sounded to me like he was telling the truth. Selman may be a rustler and a killer, but he isn't known to be a liar. Larn, maybe. But not John Selman." Cruger scuffed a toe in the dirt. "Wonder how those hides really got there?''

McLochlin's grin widened. "I haven't the foggiest notion, Sheriff Cruger," he said.

Griffin, Texas
June 1878

Shackleford County Sheriff Bill Cruger fidgeted with his coffee cup and waited for the stocky rancher seated across from him to finish tamping his pipe. Cruger didn't like the trail this conversation was riding.

J. D. McLochlin scratched a match on the underside of his desk. "Bill, it's time to do something about Larn and the Selmans." He touched the match to the pipe bowl and puffed the tobacco into action. "I want them arrested. The charge is rustling."

Cruger swallowed. His palms were sweaty, and not from the faded heat of the coffee cup. Going up against those two and their gang of gunmen was just about suicide. "Mister McLochlin, everybody in the county knows they're cow thieves. But there's no proof—"

McLochlin jabbed his pipe stem toward Cruger. "People around here haven't forgotten the Clear Fork hides, Bill. Any jury will remember them. And I've got a witness."

Cruger squirmed in his chair. "I don't have a warrant."

"I've taken care of that." McLochlin pushed back his chair, rose, and began to pace slowly in front of the fireplace. "This witness has agreed to swear out a warrant charging Larn and the Selman brothers with stealing some of his stock. It will be on your desk when you get back to Griffin. And I want the Texas Rangers kept out of it. They don't understand the situation here."

Cruger knew there was no use in arguing. McLochlin expected things done when he wanted them done. His way. "I'll need some help, Mister McLochlin."

McLochlin puffed on his pipe and squinted through the cloud of blue smoke. "You'll have it. I've some friends who have no love lost for Selman and Larn. You can count on your deputy, and on George and Ben Reynolds. They may be in-laws of Larn, but they've got a hefty dislike for him. They'll meet you tonight in the Drovers Camp. You pick a half-dozen others you can trust."

McLochlin poured two drinks from a cut-glass decanter on his desk. "Now, Bill, here's what I want you to do . . ."

A half hour later the blocky Scot watched from a window as Bill Cruger reined his horse toward Griffin. All was going according to plans laid long ago. Selman and Larn would be out of the way. They had served their purpose.

McLochlin snorted in disgust. Proof. Cruger wanted proof. *A few months on the job and he starts talking like a sheriff. Once those three are in custody, nobody will need evidence.*

Minnie Martin lounged against the bar of the Drovers Camp and strained against the crowd noise to overhear bits of conversation from the gathering of men at the table behind her. They were well into their fourth bottle now.

The talk had been muted and solemn at first; the men fell silent whenever she delivered drinks to the table. That in itself was unusual. She knew all of them, either casually or professionally—Sheriff Cruger, Deputy Dave Barker, the Reynolds brothers, William Gilson, the rancher she knew only as Treadwell, and the short, compact gunman they called Tucker. She had overheard the names Selman and Larn mentioned on several occasions, and these men at the table were certainly no friends of the two Clear Fork ranchers.

Cruger, Barker, and the Reynolds brothers pushed back their chairs and left. The meeting was breaking up. Gilson followed. Moments later Treadwell tugged on his hat and headed for the door. Tucker remained, nursing the last drink from his bottle.

Minnie gestured toward the bartender. "Two, on me," she said. She carried the glasses to the table where Tucker sat. She leaned against Tucker and smiled.

"Join me for a drink, sugar?" She leaned over to place a glass before Tucker. She saw the man's eyes widen as her dress fell open, exposing a breast. Minnie had practiced that move often. It was a basic tool of her trade.

"Miss Minnie, I'd be honored."

Minnie toed a chair close to Tucker and sat, letting her leg press against his. She raised her glass and sipped at the raw whiskey. The stocky gunman was showing the effects of his drinks. A touch of spittle clung to the edge of his mouth and he seemed to have trouble focusing his gaze, which at the moment was riveted to Minnie's chest.

"How about it, sugar?" she said. "How would you like to go upstairs with Miss Minnie? I saw you watching me earlier." She stroked his forearm. "You look like a man who could show a girl a good time." She let her hand drop to his thigh and leaned forward to whisper in his ear. "It's free tonight for you, sugar. Let's see if you're as good as you look."

Tucker swallowed, then grinned and nodded. Minnie reached for his hand. "Come along. There's a nice, soft bed upstairs."

The clock at her bedside chimed three times as Minnie cuddled Tucker's cheek against her breast. She preferred not to bed drunks. It took too long for them to get their business done despite her considerable skills, and quick work was the backbone of the prostitution trade. But she had pegged this one right. Whiskey slowed his responses, but it also loosened his tongue. Minnie didn't have all the details, but she had enough. And dawn wasn't that far away.

She nudged the drowsy Tucker. "Sorry to bother you, sugar, but you have to leave now. This girl needs her beauty rest."

Minnie forced a smile through a growing sense of urgency as Tucker fumbled his way from the bed. She almost cursed aloud at his slowness in climbing back into his clothes, but she kept the practiced smile on her face.

"You're good, sugar. Sure enough. But do me a favor, eh? Keep it quiet. I never give it away, and I'd hate for word to get around that I had. Bad for business, you know."

Tucker mumbled his agreement. Minnie unlocked the back door and waited anxiously until she heard his erratic footsteps on the stairs. Then, when she was sure he had gone, she threw on a pair of pants, shirt, and riding boots and hurried to the stable.

Outside Fort Griffin, Minnie kicked her gray mare into a long lope. She glanced anxiously at the stars. Time was short, but she had to warn Selman and Larn.

For most of his adult life John Selman had seldom slept through a sunrise. He sat now at the kitchen table alone, sipping his first morning coffee, and enjoying the predawn quiet, when the sound of a fast-moving horse penetrated the thick walls of Rock Ranch.

John swept his Colt from its holster. In two strides he was at the window, parting the curtains to peer into the semidarkness of the fading quarter moon. He recognized the rider before the horse slid to a stop outside, nostrils flared, lathered sides heaving. He stepped onto the narrow front porch.

"John!" The urgency in Minnie's voice bordered on panic.

"Here, Minnie. Trouble of some sort?"

Minnie dismounted, stumbled on legs unaccustomed to long horseback rides. "You've got to get out, John. They're coming for you. And Tom. At dawn."

"Who?"

"Vigilantes. Cruger's got a bunch of men. They're after Larn, too. I found out—early this morning." Minnie sagged against a porch railing. "I missed the road to Young John's place in the dark. They have a warrant. John, you can't let them—they'll hang you—"

"What is it, John?" Edna, her belly distended by the child she carried, stood in the doorway.

"Trouble, Edna. Big trouble." He steered the exhausted Minnie into the house, and helped her into a seat. The prostitute's eyes were bloodshot. Streaks of makeup darkened her cheeks. "Edna, take care of Minnie. Roust Tom. Tell him to bring his rifle and meet me on the bluff across from Larn's place." John grabbed both the Henry and the Sharps from the gun rack, along with several boxes of ammunition. "Minnie, your horse is worn out. I'll warn Larn."

John Selman embraced his wife. "You should be safe here. Not even a bunch of cutthroats would dare harm women or children. I'll be back as soon as I can."

Edna Selman watched the door close behind her husband. She turned to the Fort Griffin prostitute and saw her own fears reflected in Minnie Martin's eyes.

"Minnie, thank you. For warning us."

"John's a friend of mine, Missus Selman. Just a friend." Minnie had no qualms about the lie. If Edna Selman didn't know of the brief fling her husband had had with a common whore, Minnie was not going to be the one to tell her. "Out here, friends watch out for friends. John's a good man, despite what his enemies say. I couldn't bear to see him—and you—come to grief."

The clatter of hooves on hard-packed ground sounded outside. "I just pray," Minnie said softly, "that John gets to Larn's place in time."

John Larn winced as the milk cow's tail slapped him on the back of the neck. "Damn you! I'm going to tie a rock on that switch." The pail beneath the milk cow was half full. Larn's steady strokes, left hand, right hand, kept the liquid flowing in a near-constant stream.

Larn heard the soft crunch of a boot and glanced over his shoulder—into the dark bores of two handguns trained on his back. Bill Cruger and Ben Reynolds stood behind the guns.

"Just sit easy, Larn," Cruger said. "I've a warrant for your arrest. There's several men outside, so don't get any wild ideas."

John Larn studied the two men for a moment. Cruger's eyes were those of a nervous man. Ben Reynolds was smiling. "Ben," Larn said calmly, "we've had our differences, but I never thought I'd see the day you'd pull a gun on me. Doesn't seem the right thing for a man to do to his own kin."

"Kin by marriage only," Reynolds said. "You going to do something foolish, John?"

Larn knew he was in a serious bind. He didn't doubt for a moment the two would gun him down on the spot. Even if he got past them, there would be others outside; Cruger and Reynolds didn't have the guts to face him without more guns in reserve.

Larn shrugged. "I suppose not." He stood, unbuckled his gun-belt, handed the weapon to Bill Cruger, and led the way outside. Ten men waited in the corral, guns drawn.

Larn forced a grin. "I guess I can spend a little time in the Griffin lockup. Man can use a rest now and then."

"It won't be Griffin, John," Reynolds said. "We're taking you to Albany."

The smile faded from Larn's face. In Griffin he had friends. He would be out of jail before sundown. In Albany it would be a skunk of a different stink. And there was an even more pressing problem. There was nothing to stop the posse from shooting or hanging him on the way. Killed while trying to escape, they'd say.

He was no stranger to the phrase himself. He struggled to control his growing rage.

"Give me my gun back, Cruger, and we'll have it done with now," Larn snapped.

"Not a chance, Young John," Deputy Dave Barker said. There was amusement in his voice. "We've got the nest egg now. I think we'll just sit on it and see what hatches."

John Larn measured his chances. They weren't good. But there was one way he could make sure he wasn't lynched on the way to Albany.

"All right. You got the guns. But I want my wife and son to go with us."

Larn saw confusion darken Cruger's face. The sheriff hadn't planned on that development. It put him in a ticklish spot. If he refused and Larn never made it to Albany, Mary would know what really happened. Mary Matthews Larn had powerful friends; she could raise a yell that would be heard all the way to Austin. Cruger realized he was trapped. He nodded his agreement.

John Larn knew he had won at least one deal in a deadly game. He would live to see Albany. He fixed a steady stare on Ben Reynolds, then on Cruger. "When I get out of jail, you two better be halfway to Colorado." His words were bitter and deadly. "I'll see you both in hell for this."

Cruger winced at the threat, but Reynolds merely chuckled, as if at some unspoken joke.

From his vantage point on the bluff across the Clear Fork from Larn's ranch, John Selman spat a sharp curse. He had been too late.

Ten riders surrounded the wagon in which Larn, his wife and son Will, and two armed guards rode. A dozen men total, all carrying rifles or shotguns and wearing sidearms. Selman bit back his frustration and glanced at Tom, who crouched beside him, Winchester in hand. The younger Selman's eyes were cold, expressionless, as he analyzed the situation. He had reached the river bluff right behind John, his horse lathered and heaving from covering two miles at a high lope.

"We can take them, John," Tom said.

John put his hand over the breech of Tom's rifle. "No. There's too many of them."

"We can't just sit here and—"

"Do nothing?" John interrupted. "We won't, Tom. But even if we got lucky, if we dropped as many as five or six, we still wouldn't stand a chance in hell of getting Larn out of there. All we would manage to do is get him, his family, and probably ourselves killed." He glared toward the riders, now almost beyond view at a bend in the narrow, rutted road. "All we can do now is follow them. Find out where they're taking Larn. We'll cut across to the fork in the road. They take the left fork, it's Griffin. Right, it's Albany."

Less than an hour later, they had their answer. The posse took the right fork.

"All right, Tom, here's what we'll do," John said. "I'll ride on ahead, scout the town. I want you to go to Griffin. Get Jesse Evans. Four or five other good men that we know we can trust. Meet me a quarter mile north of Albany, where the low ridge cuts across the flats."

John tugged his hat down and swung into the saddle. "Tom, Albany's going to have something to talk about soon. We're going to pull the biggest jailbreak this country's ever seen."

John reined his mount toward Albany, the Henry at the ready, Sharps loaded in the saddle boot. He had recognized several of the riders in the posse that held Larn. Half were McLochlin men, including the sheriff and the deputy. "God knows," he said, "Bill Cruger hasn't got the brains or the balls to try something like this on his own."

And when John Larn was broken from the Albany jail, there would be a bloodletting in Griffin, he vowed silently.

Edna Selman swallowed against the wave of nausea and dizziness, and glared at the two men at the door of her Rock Ranch home. Four others remained mounted in the front yard.

"My husband is not here, Mister Hawsley," she snapped. "I've no idea where he might be. Or his brother." Her right hand pressed against the pain in her bloated belly.

"Missus Selman, I hate to question your word," Bill Hawsley

said, "but I've a warrant to serve. I'll have to ask you to let me search the house."

Edna stepped from the doorway. "Then search and be damned, Bill Hawsley. I've a suspicion you know he isn't here, because you don't have the courage to try to arrest John Selman face-to-face. If he *were* here, he would have killed you by now."

Hawsley's face flushed in anger. "It's a good thing you're a woman, talking to me like that—"

"I'll talk to you any way I please, *Mister* Hawsley! Now get on with it. Search. And if you *must* defile my home with your presence, the least you can do is wipe your boots before you come in!"

Hawsley grumbled and blustered, but he paused to wipe the soles of his boots on the horsehair doormat before entering the house. Edna pushed the door open. She was relieved that Minnie Martin had left just before the men arrived. Edna had no particular soft spot for prostitutes, but the woman had probably saved John's life, and for that she had earned a measure of gratitude.

Bill Hawsley reappeared at the front door moments later. "They're not here," he said to the riders. He turned to Edna. "Missus Selman, I strongly suggest that when your husband comes home, you urge him to surrender to Sheriff Cruger. The warrant—"

"Mister Hawsley," Edna interrupted, "if that is a legitimate warrant, you turn it over to Sergeant Van Riper. My husband might surrender to the rangers, but never to the likes of you. Now, get off my land."

Edna sagged against the doorjamb as the riders faded into the distance. She groaned at the fresh lance of pain across her abdomen. Something wasn't going right with this pregnancy; she had had no trouble before. Half her mind was with the unborn child, the other half with her husband—and the question both halves kept asking was simply, "Why?"

John Larn sat impassively as the Albany blacksmith drove home the final rivet in the irons clamped about his ankles.

Outside the shop a crowd had already gathered. *Didn't take long for the word to get around,* Larn mused. *Looks like most of the good folks of Albany turned out to see the famous gunman John Larn in leg irons.* He flashed a smile and a quick wave to a wide-eyed ten-year-old boy standing at the smithy's door. The boy's mother clamped a hand on the youth's shoulder and yanked him abruptly from view.

The chains clanked around Larn's feet as a half-dozen armed men escorted him to Albany's makeshift jail. The lockup was hardly more than a two-room, thin-walled shack.

Larn nodded a greeting to the three other prisoners crowded into the small room. A deputy riveted the trace chain connected to Larn's leg irons to a clamp above the fireplace, gave the chain a tug and, satisfied with his handiwork, left the room.

"What you in for, friend?" one of the prisoners asked.

"Not for long," Larn said with a grin. "My wife's gone for a lawyer." *And even if the lawyer can't do his job, it won't take Selman and the boys more than a couple minutes to take this place apart.*

An hour later a deputy stepped into the room. "Your lawyer just left, Larn. We ran him off. You might as well settle in. Looks like you'll be here for a while. Supper's in about a half hour. The grub isn't bad."

Larn shrugged. The lawyer was just one card in the deck. He still had the ace. John Selman. Larn stretched, then sat. It took him a moment to discover he could lie down on the thin pallet along the wall by the fireplace and be reasonably comfortable. Until Old John and the boys came for him—

Deputy City Marshal John Poe stretched and yawned in the room outside the cell, listening to the ragged snores of the guard he had relieved two hours ago. He checked his pocket watch. Almost midnight. Poe came to his feet at the tap on the door. He twisted his key in the lock, peered at the men outside, and swung the door open. He had been expecting them.

Ten men clad in slickers pulled bandanas over their faces as they strode into the makeshift jail. All carried rifles. One of them poked a gun muzzle in the sleeping guard's ribs and silently motioned the groggy man to join Poe, who stood by the door, hands raised.

Nine of the masked men walked to the door of the cell room while the tenth kept his rifle on the guards.

John Larn, awake on the hard pallet, chuckled to himself. From the sound of things outside, Old John and the boys had arrived. He stood.

The nine men crowded into the small cell, rifle muzzles trained on Larn's body. Selman was not among them. John Larn then knew he was facing his executioners. A quiet calm settled over him.

"John Larn," one of the men said, "in recognition of some of your better qualities, we are not going to hang you."

The smile returned to Larn's face. "Do the job right, then. John Larn takes a lot of killing."

The sharp cracks of the rifle volley slammed through the quiet streets of Albany.

Atop the low hill at the outskirts of Albany, John Selman felt the rifle blasts tear through his own gut. "The bastards! The murdering bastards!" He picked up his rifle and started to rise. A firm hand on his shoulder pushed him back to the chill earth.

"Let it go, Selman," Jesse Evans said. "We can't help Young John now. No need you getting killed, too."

"Jesse's right, John," Tom Selman added. "Larn's dead. We can't change that. We can make them pay, but not now." He jabbed his rifle muzzle toward Albany below. Lights flared in windows, doors swung open, armed men poured into the streets. "There's a hundred guns down there, John. You've been chewing my butt for years to think before I shoot. This time you better listen to your own advice."

John Selman felt a tightness grip his throat. "Dammit, I should have moved sooner." He had to force the words. "I killed him just as sure as those cowards did."

"No, John." Tom's voice was soft in the deep velvet of the moonless night. "Larn just ran out of time. Now let's get out of here. We still have to stay alive ourselves."

The sun was still low in the eastern sky when the Albany coroner's inquest returned its verdict on the slaying of John Larn: Death by gunshot wounds fired by parties unknown.

Edna Selman clenched her fists on the arms of her husband's chair beside the fireplace, and waited for the screeching pain in her abdomen to subside.

The nausea was almost constant now. It stalked her through the night, denied her rest, refused to let her take nourishment. The sickness and pain combined to drain what little strength she had left. Seeing to the basic needs of her children was almost more than she could handle.

Henry, her firstborn, was nine now, William eight. The two boys were helpful, caring for the horses and such household chores as they could handle. Margaretta, at six, sensed that something was wrong and spent most of her waking hours at her mother's side. Two-year-old John Junior was simply too young to be aware of anything other than himself.

Fear and uncertainty added to Edna's misery. She did not know when, or if, she would see John and Tom again, or where they were now. She kept trying to fight back the one image that insisted on forming in her mind, that of the two men lying dead on the windswept prairie.

Edna wiped the cold sweat from her brow with the sleeve of her house dress. Through the east window she could see the first rays of the new day break through low clouds—and the glint of sunlight on metal.

The window exploded. Shards of glass spun into the room. Edna felt the sting of a cut along her cheek before she heard the sound of the gunshot. A second slug hammered into the house and thudded into a back wall, followed by a third and a fourth. Through the surprise and shock, Edna realized the house was under attack.

"Henry, William! Get the young ones under the bed!" Edna took a step toward the shotgun hanging by the door, then went down on hands and knees as a rifle ball ripped through a thin wood door panel and whipped past her head. Over the roar of the rifles, the sound of glass and plates smashing, the whump of slugs into walls and furniture, she heard John Junior's terrified wail. *God, the babies.* A sob broke through the terror that clutched at her throat. Edna crawled to the bedroom and placed her body in front of the children huddled beneath the bed.

The roar of the rifles stopped. The sudden silence was broken only by the baby's cries, and then the tinkle of glass as a mirror toppled and shattered.

"John Selman!" The call came from near the doorway. "Come on out! We have the place surrounded!"

Edna lay gasping for breath, unable to speak or move. William

Selman scrambled from beneath the bed, evading Edna's grasp, and ran to the door.

"My father's not here!" William yelled, his voice quavering. "My mother's sick! Go away! Leave us alone!" William reached on tiptoes for the long-barreled shotgun racked beside the door, and tried to pull the hammers back with one hand.

The bullet-riddled door swung open.

A man in a yellow slicker, a blue bandana covering his face except for his eyes, stepped into the room, pistol in hand. William raised the shotgun. The man in the slicker knocked the barrel aside with his gun, and with his free hand slammed a backhand blow alongside William's face. The shotgun fell as the boy sprawled on the floor.

Edna heaved herself to her knees and crabbed toward the crumpled form. Tears streamed openly down her face.

"Damn you! Damn you to hell!" Edna knelt at William's side. The boy stirred, then moaned. "You could have killed my babies!"

The man in the slicker did not reply. Another man, similarly clad, appeared in the doorway, the muzzle of his rifle pointed toward Edna. The first gunman moved quickly from room to room, then returned. "Not here," he said simply.

Edna's tearful helplessness exploded into rage, pushing aside the pain in her belly. She heaved herself to her feet, flung herself at the man with the rifle, fingers raking at his face, drawing blood. The man grabbed her with his free hand and roughly pushed her down.

"Let's get out of here, Jake. I didn't plan on makin' no war against women and kids," the first gunman said.

The man called Jake glared at Edna. Blood welled in the scratches beside his eye. For a moment Edna thought he would shoot her. Then he slowly backed from sight through the doorway.

A moment later the sound of hoofbeats moving away reached Edna's ears. William struggled, still groggy, and lurched to his feet. "Are you—all right—Mother?"

Edna pulled the boy to her. "I'm all right, William." A massive bruise was forming over the side of William's face. "That was a brave thing you did, William."

"I was too slow—too small." Frustration and fear were visible in William's tear-streaked face.

Edna's quick check showed none of the children were seriously injured. The house was a shambles, but that was nothing—Edna gasped and doubled over in agony. It was as if a razor had slashed through her lower belly.

"William, I—get your horse—get Uncle Jasper—and doctor. Please—please hurry."

Jesse Evans rode into John Selman's camp in a narrow, wooded canyon along a bend in the Red River. The first rays of the sun were touching the top of the clay-colored bluffs above.

John Selman sat at a makeshift table in the old one-room adobe shack, which had been abandoned years before by a wandering Mexican sheepherder. John wiped an oiled rag over the magazine of the Henry.

"John, I've got some bad news," Evans said. "I just came from the deGraffenreid place. Edna died three days ago."

In the pale dawn light that filtered through the roofless shack, Jesse Evans saw the color drain from his friend's face. John Selman stared for a long moment at Jesse. The expression in the pale blue eyes was one of disbelief. The vacant look gave way to the pinched face of a man in agony.

Tom Selman turned from the crumbling rock fireplace where he tended a coffee pot. "How, Jesse? What happened?"

Jesse Evans, who feared few men and fewer animals, had to force himself to look into John Selman's eyes. "The baby came too soon. It was born dead. The doctor couldn't stop the bleeding. Edna died an hour later." Evans scuffed a toe in the dirt of the floorless shack.

John Selman stared wordlessly past Evans for several minutes. Then he stood and shuffled out the door, shoulders slumped, his rifle forgotten on the table.

Evans watched him go, wishing he could have spared John somehow. But John had to know. Evans glanced at Tom. "What do we do now, Tom Cat? What can we say to him?"

Tom turned back to the coffee pot bubbling on the small fire. "Nothing, Jesse. It's best to leave him alone right now. Man's got a right to hurt in his own way."

Tom Cat Selman wrapped a rag around the handle of the coffee pot and filled a tin cup for Evans. He paused, looked past the door toward a distant outcropping of rock where a solitary figure sat, staring toward the river below.

"When his hurt's eased, Jesse, there's going to be pure hell to pay along the Clear Fork of the Brazos."

McLochlin Ranch
June 1878

John Selman dug his elbows into the depressions of the shallow shooting pit, which was set behind a fallen log near the cottonwood grove a hundred yards from the McLochlin ranch headquarters. He rested the barrel of the Sharps on a blanket draped across the log and waited.

For three days and nights he had lain in wait for a clear shot at the stocky rancher. When the game was spooked the hunt was tougher.

McLochlin was spooked.

He had good reason to be.

The McLochlin stable of gunmen was dwindling. The one called Daley had caught a large-caliber rifle slug between the eyes a week ago. Two days later, John had caught Jake—the one with the scratches on his face—alone. The scratches were gone now, along with most of Jake's head. Six rounds from a Colt, in the back of the head at close range, tended to wipe out a lot of things.

A third McLochlin man from the posse that had captured John Larn lay in a shallow ravine, half his ribs blown away by three Sharps slugs.

McLochlin knew his name was on the list as well. He seldom ventured outside without taking at least three gunmen along. Twice he had sent groups of riders out on scout. They were gunmen, not trackers, and John had no difficulty avoiding them. Search parties from Griffin had passed within fifty yards three times without cutting his trail.

John Selman was a patient hunter. He could outwait the Scot. His shooting pit, dug in the manner preferred by buffalo hunters and the snipers of the Civil War, gave him a clear view of the path between the main ranch house and the small outhouse in the back yard.

A man could change a lot of things in his life, Selman knew, but there was one thing in which most men were total creatures of habit—the time of day they answered nature's call.

McLochlin's trips to the outhouse had been in the company of his three bodyguards for the past couple of days. But this morning, four ML riders had saddled up at first light and ridden off toward the west. John had counted on that eventuality. McLochlin couldn't keep all his guns around all the time, or he wouldn't have a ranch to run. Now, only Everett remained with McLochlin.

John glanced at the new Winchester he had taken from Daley's body. The weapon lay at his side, hammer cocked, magazine full. It would take only a second to bring it into play after the Sharps thundered its one time. John had sighted in the Winchester to his own needs and found it a deadly accurate piece.

The back door of the ranch house swung open. Everett came out, rifle at the ready, glanced around and then apparently called to McLochlin waiting just inside. The rancher stepped into the back yard alongside Everett and started toward the outhouse thirty paces away.

John snugged the Sharps against his shoulder, his cheek nestled against the familiar wood of the stock, and eased the hammer back to full cock. The front sight post slipped into the center of the narrow V of the tang sight. The two blurred slightly, forming a single entity centered on the side of McLochlin's head as he walked toward the privy.

John took a deep breath and exhaled slowly. His finger tightened on the trigger.

The Sharps bellowed and slammed against his shoulder. John sensed, rather than saw, the massive slug tear through McLochlin's head. The smoke cleared a second later. McLochlin lay in the dirt, legs twitching in reflex even though the brain was already dead.

John scooped up the Winchester as Everett crouched and turned toward the cottonwood grove. John shot him in the chest, levered the rifle, and packed a second bullet almost atop the first.

The impact knocked Everett backward and spun him around. John put a third shot into the rider's back as he went down.

John Selman waited until the echoes of the rifle fire died away. He studied the bodies for a few moments until he was satisfied both men were dead.

Then he reloaded the Sharps, shouldered both rifles, and began the half-mile walk to the tree-studded canyon where his horse and pack animal waited.

John gave little thought to the possibility of pursuit. The other McLochlin riders would have been several miles away from the ranch by the time he cut the Sharps loose. And even if they had heard the shots, John was reasonably sure they would be in no particular rush to track him down. If they came after him, it would cost them. Both Selman and the riders knew it.

The sun was barely three fingers above the eastern horizon as John Selman snubbed the lead rope of the pack horse into the rear cinch ring of his saddle, and kneed his mount toward the east.

"Guess it's time for us to get clear of this country," he told the horse. The sorrel's ears twitched in response to the familiar voice.

John knew the country would be crawling with rangers and members of McLochlin's vigilante group now. It was time to quit the hunt.

Jesse Evans and Tom Cat Selman would be waiting on the New Mexico side of the great Staked Plains, in Lincoln.

FIVE

Lincoln, New Mexico
July 1878

John Selman ducked behind the sandbagged wagon bed as slugs screamed overhead and ripped into the barricade across from Alex McSween's home. He chanced a glance through a crack in the bulwark.

John Long ran through the barrage of lead fired from the house, cursing at every step as bullets kicked dust at his heels. He vaulted head-first over the edge of the overturned wagon, rolled a couple of times, then scrambled back to safety between Jessie Evans and John Selman, who were among two dozen gunmen crouched behind the barricade.

"Dammit!" Long's chest heaved with exertion. "You guys were supposed to cover me!"

"We did," Evans said with a grin. "We ducked behind all the cover we could find." Evans lifted his rifle and slapped a shot toward the McSween house.

The echoes of gunfire rattled through the streets of Lincoln. A wisp of smoke drifted from a shattered window of the house, then stopped.

John Long muttered a string of cuss words.

Evans winked at Selman. "Old John, I never thought I'd see the day we'd be throwing in with a man can't even start a fire. What kind of outlaws they raise in New Mexico, anyway?"

Long glared at Evans. "You so damn smart, *you* burn 'em out." All three men flinched as a rifle ball nicked a sandbag six inches from Long's face and whirred away. The shot triggered another volley from the gunmen along the barricade. Slivers of wood flew from the McSween house. Selman heard the tinkle of glass as the one remaining window shattered.

"I'll burn the bastards out next time," Long grumbled. "But I'm gonna wait till dark. Those rannies shoot a tad too good for my taste."

The gunfire died to sporadic outbursts. A few feet to John Selman's left, a rifleman raised his head to take aim, then flopped back, wiping at a raw burn on his cheek.

"Musta been the Kid let that one loose," Evans said. "Bucktoothed little fart can fair shoot."

John Selman grunted. William Bonney, alias Billy the Kid, wasn't the only one in the McSween house who could handle a gun.

For five days now the standoff at the McSween house had continued. Inside, the group calling themselves the Regulators, led by young Billy, had a good field of fire from the second-floor windows. Outside, the Seven Rivers Warriors, with Long in control, had a solid barricade for defense, more men, and supposedly the law on their side. They had been sworn in as deputies by Sheriff Dad Peppin.

John Selman had joined the Warriors just before the siege opened. He didn't know and didn't care which side was right in McSween's feud with the Dolan-Riley band, the dispute that had triggered the Lincoln County Range War. He was a gun for hire. That, and the fact that Jesse Evans and Tom Cat Selman were Warriors, were enough for John Selman.

John knew the Warriors were in for a long fight. The Kid and his Regulators weren't about to surrender. None of them were overly anxious to hang. And Long's men couldn't storm the house without paying a heavy price in blood.

Now, Peppin and Long had decided the only way to dislodge the Regulators was to burn them out before the army decided to step in and put an end to the battle.

Neither side had suffered many casualties, despite the amount of powder that had been burned. A couple of Regulators had been hit, and the Warriors had one dead and one wounded. Most of the killing was already over by the time John had ridden into Lincoln.

The scorching New Mexico sun finally dropped behind the

western hills. Long waited until full darkness covered the streets, then slipped through an opening in the barricade and sprinted for the McSween house.

Selman watched, rifle at the ready. Tom Cat was now at his side. A torch flared inside the first floor of the house. "By God," Tom Cat muttered, "Long may have done the job this time."

The fire was spreading rapidly when Long returned on the run, darting first one way and then another as gun muzzles flamed from the windows. John waited until a second flash erupted from a certain window, then hammered a shot toward the muzzle blast. Shooting by firelight was chancy at best; he had no idea where his shot had gone.

He had little time to worry about it.

The sharp crack of rifles and handguns and the deeper cough of shotguns broke like a thunderstorm as the gunmen in the house fled the flames. John levered fresh rounds into the Winchester and fired as rapidly as he could point the muzzle and pull. It was impossible to fire a well-aimed shot; smoke obscured most of the light from the blazing home. John saw a man who fit McSween's description try to escape through the front door. He was cut down in a storm of lead. Another Regulator tumbled through a side window, staggered under the impact of a slug, then disappeared into the darkness.

After ten minutes of almost continuous firing, the Warrior guns fell silent one by one, left with no more targets. The shouts of men mixed with the crackle of timber in the inferno that had been the McSween house.

By first light, the streets of Lincoln were once again quiet. McSween and another of his Regulators were dead. The Kid and most of his followers had escaped in the confusion and darkness. The Warriors had two men slightly injured in the final clash. John sensed that Long's band had won the skirmish. Maybe the Lincoln County War as well.

John Long apparently felt the same.

"Well, gents, looks like the fun's over." He glanced down the street toward the middle of town. "I think we best find other pastures to graze. The locals seem a tad put out with us. Just a matter of time until they convince the army to come callin'."

"What do we do now, Long?" one of the riders asked.

Long scratched an itch behind his right ear. "Split up for now in case the army gets pulled in on us." He laughed aloud. "Hell, boys. Ain't nothin' much in New Mexico. Nothin' but stock to be rustled, banks to be robbed, *señorita* skirts to be lifted, and whiskey to be drunk. No law to speak of. Man couldn't want more." Long sighed wistfully. "God, it's going to be good to get back to honest work again. Politics is a real pain in the butt."

Seven Rivers
August 1878

John and Tom Cat Selman, Reese Gobles, Gus Owens, Charlie Snow, and Bob Speakes herded the hundred head of stolen cattle toward a shallow, steep-walled canyon along the banks of the Pecos. There, money would change hands and the cattle would be driven downriver to Horsehead Crossing, then east to stock a new ranch in the Texas Hill Country.

Since John Selman had decided that, by God, if Texas wanted him to be an outlaw he'd be one of the best, he had discovered an astonishingly easy market for rustled cattle. Especially those from John Chisum's herd. Chisum had plenty. He'd never miss a few dozen head from time to time.

The buyer was waiting in the quarter-mile-wide mouth of the canyon. John suppressed a grin. The buyer was a member of one of Central Texas's most prominent ranching families. John wondered who the real thief was, himself or the young man in the silk shirt who had built a fortune and a political power base on other men's cows.

John let his gaze drift over the pine- and cedar-studded walls of the river breaks. The Seven Rivers country was ideal for the lawless breed. The long, broad valley where tributaries wandered into the Pecos River held prime grass and plenty of water. It was within three days' ride of the fine stock on the Chisum ranch or on the spread that had belonged to John Tunstall, whose murder had ignited the Lincoln County War. Tunstall didn't need the cattle now.

Small communities, fruit farms, isolated ranch houses, and

trading posts dotted the hundred-plus miles of the Seven Rivers drainage area and followed the Pecos another two hundred miles downstream. Easy pickings for men good with a gun and not particular about who they stole from.

Best of all, it was a land the law couldn't—or wouldn't—touch. Canyons, breaks, badlands, and timber held places a band of men could hide. And if that still wasn't enough, there were mountains within an easy ride. In the Capitans, Jicarillas, White Mountain, or Sacramento ranges, an army regiment could camp undetected. A man in this business couldn't ask for better, John thought.

John offered a handshake to the buyer, folded the stack of bills into a shirt pocket, and watched as Tom and the others trailed the stock along the river. The buyer's drovers would take over a couple miles downstream. It was one of the terms of a Selman deal. No buyer or even a cowboy saw John's headquarters or had a chance to count the guns in the Seven Rivers band. In return, no one knew the true identity of the buyer except John Selman. It was a comfortable business arrangement all around.

John reined his horse toward the main outlaw camp and the problem that awaited him there.

The problem's name was Hart. If he had a first name, John had never heard it. Hart was supposed to be the leader of the group John rode with, but he was usually drunk or tumbling with his Mexican whore when there was work to be done or guns to be faced. And John was the first to admit he just plain didn't like the man. Hart, a swarthy, broad-faced man with bad teeth, seldom missed a chance to brag about his ability with a gun. As far as John knew, Hart had killed only once—an unarmed, retarded boy Hart shot in the back during a raid on a farm outside Roswell.

John knew the Warriors he rode with accepted him, not Hart, as the true leader. He had a feeling Hart sensed it too, despite Hart's insistence that he was the only boss. John knew it was only a matter of time until the two clashed to settle the matter. He also knew Hart wasn't going to be the one with the full hand when the time came.

An hour later John sat at a pine table in the center of the adobe house the Warriors had established as their headquarters. He had started separating the pile of bills into shares when Tom Cat and the others rode up. Hart sat down across from John, a scowl on his face and a half-empty bottle in his hand.

"Dammit, Selman," Hart growled, "is that all you got for them cattle?"

It looked like it was going to be one of those nights. "That's a fair price, Hart," he said, keeping his tone calm. "You think you can do better, get off your butt and do it."

Hart glared at John, then took another hefty slug from the bottle. "You should've just shot the bastard, took the money, and kept the stock."

John shrugged. He pushed Hart's share across the table and let his hands fall into his lap. He eased his Colt from its holster. "Bad for business, doing it that way. Kill one good buyer, you lose them all."

Tom Cat and Reese Gobles sauntered into the room, the garrulous Reese halfway through an off-color story. Reese's voice trailed off as he glanced first at Hart, then at John, and felt the tension in the air.

"Selman," Hart said, "I'm gettin' a little tired of taking all this crap off you."

"I reckon the same could be said here, Hart," John replied. Beneath the table he tilted the muzzle of the Colt upward. "Guess it's time you moved on," he said. He cocked the hammer and pulled the trigger in one smooth motion. The heavy slug ripped upward through the pine table, plowed into the bridge of Hart's nose, and spattered gore over the back wall and ceiling of the adobe. Hart tumbled backward.

Tom Cat Selman nodded toward the body. "About time you shot that bastard."

The other Seven Rivers men came on the run, guns drawn. Hart's Mexican whore ran into the room, half dressed, and wailed in grief as she threw herself across Hart's body.

John ignored the body, the whore's cries, and all but one of the Seven Rivers riders. He wrapped his thumb around the hammer of the revolver and glared at Reese Gobles.

"Gobles, he was your friend," John said. "You of a mind to settle the score for him, let's get on with it."

Gobles half smiled, lifting his hands well away from his waist and the Remington revolvers he carried cross-draw style. "He wasn't friend enough to get killed over, Selman. I ain't that loyal. And I sure as hell ain't no fool. You the undisputed stud hoss around here now. Just yell 'frog' and I'll be the first one to jump.''

John held Reese Gobles's gaze for a five-count, then shrugged. He lifted the Colt, ejected the spent cartridge case, and thumbed in a fresh load before dropping the weapon into his holster. "All right, Reese." John reminded himself to keep a close eye on Gobles. The man wasn't above popping a man in the back. John glanced around. *Come to think of it, there isn't a man here wouldn't shoot somebody in the back. Myself included.*

Hart's whore was still squawling and sobbing. "Shut up, Maria," John barked. The racket stopped. Maria wiped the back of a hand across her runny nose and peered at John.

"Well, John," Tom Cat said casually, "looks like you've inherited a woman along with old Hart's other worldly goods."

John snorted in disgust. "Hell, I don't want her. Gobles, you got a taste for Mexican women with big tits. She's yours."

"Gracias, Selman," Gobles said with a slight bow.

John waved a hand. *Gobles,* he thought, *you may not be thanking me in a few weeks. Only God and a good doctor knows what might be under that skirt. With luck you might still be able to piss by the next full moon.* Reese Gobles took the woman's elbow and led her toward the back room. Maria's bereavement would be brief.

"Charlie, you and Bob do me a favor and get rid of that thing," John said with a nod toward Hart's body. "Bury it, burn it, or just throw it out in the creek for the coyotes. I don't care."

John watched as Tom Cat set about stirring the blaze in the crumbling fireplace. It was Tom's turn to cook supper. It was the rule that a man never criticized the cook, but John was glad he wasn't overly hungry. Tom Cat could handle a gun as well as anybody, and was better with horses than most, but he never had gotten the hang of iron skillets and Dutch ovens. Judging from the grunts in the other room, Maria wouldn't be any help. But that didn't matter. She wasn't even as good a cook as Tom. They'd tried her cooking once. All of them had the trots for two days. Maria damn near accomplished in one meal what half the lawmen in New Mexico had given up on—doing away with the Seven Rivers crowd.

John listened as Tom whistled, off-key, and remembered how

Edna used to hum songs from the Baptist hymnal as she cooked. The memory opened the cut in his heart again. *God, I miss her, and the kids.* The children would be fine in Jasper deGraffenreid's care, John knew, but the knowledge didn't fill the hole in his gut. *Come spring, I'll make permanent arrangements for them.*

John lifted his Winchester from its place at his side and rubbed a spot from the blue-gray receiver with an oiled rag. It was something to do.

He couldn't shake the thoughts of his family from his mind. Henry would be ten now, William almost nine. It seemed he hadn't seen them for years instead of months. So much had happened since things had blown up in Griffin.

John knew he couldn't go back home. The Clear Fork of the Brazos might as well run through the middle of New York City as far as John were concerned. There would be warrants for his arrest, maybe on murder charges in addition to the original warrant for rustling. But someday he would have a home again, have his kids with him. Patience was something a man in this business needed.

The outlaw game, John Selman decided, was overrated. The money wasn't bad. He could make in a good day what most cowboys put in six month's hard work for. But in New Mexico, the competition was fierce. John Long was running his own gang over by Lincoln, Billy the Kid had his wild bunch left over from the Regulators, and a half-dozen other outlaw bands roamed the forests and rivers. It was getting to the point, John grumbled to himself, that a man had to scout around to see what hadn't already been stolen before hitting a place.

Charlie Snow and Bob Speakes strode into the adobe, brushing dirt from their clothes. "Buried Hart down by the old juniper tree on the creek," Speakes said. "He was a sorry bastard, but I couldn't see leaving him for the coyotes."

"Good enough," John said. "Get the rest of the boys in. We'll divvy up Hart's share of the money. Tom will have supper ready in fifteen minutes. Tomorrow, saddle up your best horses. We've got some hard riding to do."

Lincoln, New Mexico
September 1878

John Selman's Seven Rivers band had cut a wide swath through New Mexico in just over a month's time. Almost a dozen men lay dead in the path they had taken—farmers, small ranchers, orchard owners, teamsters. Some were miserly store owners like Avery Clenny, whose place Selman's gang had looted and then practically demolished. They hadn't killed Clenny. He was one of the few they hadn't. There weren't many witnesses left to identify the men from Seven Rivers.

For most of the dead men, John had no feelings of remorse. The boys bothered him a bit. The Mexican boy Reese Gobles had shot down on a watermelon farm. The two Chavez youths who had been stupid enough to argue when the Seven Rivers men came for their horses. And, most of all, the half-wit who had been with the Chavez boys. The kid had no weapon. He was just standing there, crying, when Rustling Bob Irwin put a bullet in his forehead. That killing had reminded John of the incident with Jocko the half-wit and the hanging tree south of Fort Davis so long ago. Even death seemed to trigger memories of home.

Irwin and Gobles liked to kill just for the sport of it, and Selman found himself hard-pressed to keep some measure of control over the two. They were good men on the trail and fearless in a fight. They were just gun-crazy.

The Seven Rivers band had accumulated a fair-sized herd of horses and a wagonload of goods, held on the flats outside Lincoln now by Tom Cat and Bob Speakes, and their saddlebags were heavy with silver. It had been a good month.

But all the shooting had left the riders low on powder and lead. That had brought them to the outskirts of Lincoln and the home of Isaac Ellis, dealer in weapons and ammunition.

John shucked his Winchester from the saddle boot, levered a cartridge home, and kneed his gelding into a trot toward the Ellis house. A dozen men fanned out behind him and to either side. It would be a simple, straight-out robbery. Just move in, load up on ammunition and any cash lying around, and leave. Gobles and Irwin were under strict orders not to shoot unless shot at, unless they wished to answer in person to John Selman.

The Ellis place looked all but deserted as the riders closed to within twenty yards.

"That's far enough, Selman!" The call from the house caught John by surprise. Not that many people in New Mexico knew him by his real name, or even by sight. He'd worked hard to keep it that way. "Turn your bunch around and get out!"

John instinctively checked his horse. At his side, Jake Owens snorted. "Aw, hell, John. We own the damn country. Ain't no-body goin' to stand up against us." Owens kicked his horse into a lope.

A volley of rifle fire slammed from the Ellis house. Owens's horse staggered. A slug cracked past John's ear. John heard the whop of lead against flesh, and a rider on his right flank grunted in pain. The would-be charge ended in a melee of frightened horses and confused riders. Owens kicked free of the saddle as his horse went down. He fired two rounds at the house, then swung up behind another rider.

John jerked his horse around. "Get the hell out of here!" he shouted over the rattle of gunfire. "They must have an army in there!"

The Seven Rivers group faltered for a confused moment. Reese Gobles battled to control his pitching horse stung by a bullet, then got the animal lined out. A minute later the Seven Rivers riders were falling back, pausing to fire at the house.

A dozen mounted riders spilled from behind the Ellis place, whooping and firing revolvers at the cluster of outlaws. The Seven Rivers riders drove spurs into their horses in full flight. A hammer blow to John's left hip almost knocked him from the saddle. He felt the sticky wetness of his own blood at his waist before the first stab of pain laced through shocked muscles and nerves.

The outlaw band swept past their wagon toward the herd of stolen horses. Tom Cat and Bob Speakes spun their mounts toward the riders, weapons drawn.

"Forget the horses!" John yelled. "Leave the wagon! We've got to get out of here!"

Waves of pain and nausea hammered through John's body with each thud of his horse's hooves on the prairie. The gang forgot about fighting back, and ran for their lives as their pursuers tried to close in on them.

John's insistence on mounting his men with the best horses available now paid off. The gap between the two groups of men steadied, then began to slowly widen. The chase lasted fifteen miles before the Lincoln posse finally gave up and turned back.

The Seven Rivers men eased their exhausted mounts to a walk and after three more miles came to a halt. For the first time, John was able to check on his wound. A rifle slug had ripped through the cantle of his saddle and torn across the hip bone.

Tom Cat Selman examined the wound and whistled in wonder. "You got lucky, John. Bullet glanced off the hip bone instead of driving through. Been a few inches higher and right, or it hadn't hit the saddle first, you'd have left a kidney back there. Might have a cracked hip bone as it is. Hurt much?"

"It's sure as hell got my attention," John grumbled through clenched teeth. He winced as Tom pressed a bandana over the gash. "Anybody else hurt?"

"Tyler caught one in the back. He's already coughing up blood. He won't see the sun come up. Owens took a slug through the calf. He'll be all right. Couple others got lead burns or nicks, but nothing serious."

John ground his teeth as a fresh blast of pain lanced through his side and down his leg. After a moment the wave peaked and began to subside. The loss of the wagon and the horse herd pained him almost as much as the wound.

John took two swallows from the pint bottle Tom handed him. He winced as the raw tequila hit his stomach, then waited for it to take the edge off the pain. "We've got to make camp soon. The horses are worn out and we've got some healing to do." John sighed. "Dammit, Tom, this country's getting downright inhospitable."

New Mexico
October 1878

John Selman was getting a little tired of New Mexico.

The easy pickings of earlier in the year were tough as a prickly pear these days. It seemed to John as if the whole state were after the Seven Rivers Warriors. Even the army had chased them for a while, but that wasn't the big problem.

The Seven Rivers band had taken a beating in the Ellis raid. They had buried Tyler in that first night's dry camp. The next day Jake Owens and three of his friends had cut for safer pastures. For a time there were only nine Warriors left.

Then Gus Gildea and three others had joined the remnants of the Seven Rivers gang. Gildea promptly dubbed the organization Selman's Scouts, over John's weak objections. The wiry little gunman with the bushy mustache now rode at John's side as a valued lieutenant. Other men had ridden in to cast their lot with the Scouts, and now the band numbered almost twenty.

The wound in John's hip still pained him when he rode. The chronic lack of ammunition and supplies also stung. They still had a fair amount of money, but a man couldn't eat gold or shoot silver. Well, John told himself as he led his men down the road along the Hondo River, they would soon solve that problem. A few miles to the south were rich communities to be raided; trading posts, ranches, and farms to be plundered. The Scouts would soon be back at full strength, with bellies and Winchesters stocked for the long winter ahead.

John pulled his horse to a stop as the group rounded a bend in the road. Up ahead, rifle and shotgun barrels protruded from a man-made deadfall where tree limbs, rocks, and an overturned wagon bed blocked the road.

"What the hell?" Tom Cat Selman asked as he cocked his Winchester.

"John Selman!" The call from the roadblock carried a Mexican accent and the ring of authority. "Turn around and take your bandits somewhere else! You're not going another step along this road!"

"Who's going to stop us?"

"A couple of dozen New Mexicans who say you've stolen your last horse and killed your last man on the South Pecos! Look around, Selman!"

John twisted in the saddle and studied the hills which climbed close along the road. Within seconds he counted a half-dozen rifles in the rocks above. He slumped in the saddle, then turned to the riders. Several of them also were staring at the hills. There wasn't a man among them, especially John Selman, who didn't know he might be looking at his last rock. One wrong move now and the whole of the Scouts would be dead in the middle of a dusty road.

"Turn 'em around, boys," John said. "Put the guns up. They got us cold." John started to rein his horse about.

"Another thing, Selman," the unseen Mexican called from the deadfall. "You better make some tracks out of New Mexico. Juan Patron's getting some men together. He's coming after you."

John heard Gus Gildea's low curse. The dark-eyed little gun-man glared toward the roadblock. "John," Gildea said, his tone deadly serious, "if that greaser is right, we're in a mess of trouble. Patron's a bulldog on the trail and bad news with a rifle. I'd rather tangle with a division of cavalry any day than that *grandee*."

"We'll worry about this Patron later, Gus," John said. "Right now, let's see if we can't back out of this wreck. Slow and easy, so nobody gets an itch on a trigger . . ."

New Mexico
November 1878

John Selman turned in the saddle, glanced at the back-trail, and swore in English, Spanish, and as many Indian tongues as he could recall.

Juan Patron was still there.

"Dammit, Gus," John grumbled to the man at his side, "how come you have to be right all the time?" He dug spurs into his tired mount and shivered in the sharp north wind. He couldn't remember ever having been so cold.

Patron and his group had trailed them for fifteen days and more than a hundred miles, and he had bloodied the Scouts. John had lost two men in a firefight between Lloyd's Crossing and Fort Sumner, and three more in a bloody clash near Puerto de Luna. And still Patron came.

There was no rest for the Scouts. No fresh horses, no hot grub, seldom a chance to even warm themselves by a small fire. They rode and tried to hide, gnawed on jerky, rode some more. Five of the Scouts tried to steal fresh horses at a ranch in the Three Rivers country. Patron outguessed John again. John could only watch from a distance as his men were surrounded by Patron's posse, trussed like pigs on a spit, and led away toward the nearest jail.

Selman's force had been cut to less than half in just over two weeks' time. They were down to a dozen rounds of ammunition each and sore necks from watching their back-trails.

Ice crusted the edges of John's mustache. He was sure he would never be able to feel his toes again. He winced as a pellet of sleet drove into his forehead. Ahead, at the mouth of the canyon, a gray wall seemed to fill the pass.

Gus pointed toward the gray mass. A wide grin spread over the dark face, bringing fresh blood to freeze on Gildea's cracked lips. "Snowstorm," he yelled above the howl of the wind. *"Madre de Dios,* maybe we get out of this yet, Selman!"

The snow slammed down in a white blanket. John could barely make out the blurred shapes of the remaining Scouts only a dozen yards up the trail. He felt like shouting in relief. He glanced behind him. Already the snow was building in the hollows left by their horses' hooves.

The early-season snowstorm and its howling winds covered the trail of Selman's Scouts as they shivered through the pass and onto the hardpan of the lower country, and slogged toward Bosque Grande.

The snow did in two hours what none of Selman's trail skill could do in more than two weeks. Patron gave up the chase. *But he did what he set out to do,* John thought with grudging admiration. *There aren't enough of us left to rob a Chihuahua whorehouse.*

Bosque Grande, New Mexico

John Selman glowered at Reese Gobles across the pine table in the Scouts' winter camp. The game was five-card draw, jacks or better to open, and Gobles was having an uncommon run of luck.

John knew it wasn't luck.

Tom Cat lounged against the wall behind John, watching the play. Rustling Bob Irwin was at Gobles's right, a sizeable pile of bills and silver before him. Most of the money had been John Selman's two hours ago.

"Call." John tossed a five-dollar bill on the table. He let his right hand drop below the table and eased his Colt from its holster.

"Four queens," Gobles said as he fanned his hand on the table. "My pot." He reached for the money.

"Four queens is damn curious, Reese." John kept his tone even, trying to hide his growing anger. "Damn curious, because I discarded a queen on the draw."

Gobles's swarthy face reddened. His eyes narrowed as he stared at John. "What are you sayin'?"

John reached out with his left hand, flipped over the discards, and fanned them out. The queen of clubs was near the center of the fan. "I'm saying you're a pure fool, Gobles. And not a very good card cheat."

"Damn you, Selman!" Gobles half stood, clawing at the gun in his waistband. John thumbed the Colt and fired. Gobles took the heavy slug square in the chest and fell backward in a clatter of coins and chair. John swung the pistol toward Irwin. Before he could thumb the hammer and fire, the side of Irwin's head exploded.

John glanced at Tom. A wisp of smoke drifted from the revolver in Tom's fist. "Been watching Irwin," Tom said, his tone matter-of-fact. "He was in on it, too. Thought you might need a hand."

John's ears rang from the concussion of the muzzle blast of

Tom Cat's Colt. "Obliged, Tom. Bastards deserved killing whether they were cheating or not."

"What do we do with them?"

John scooped the money from the table and tucked it into his shirt pocket. "We'll drag 'em outside—" He raised a hand for silence as the pound of horse's hooves sounded outside the remote cabin.

John leveled his handgun at the door.

"John, Tom!" Gus Gildea's voice cut through the high-pitched ringing in John's ears. "Everything all right in there?"

"Come on in, Gus." John lowered the hammer on the Colt and dropped the weapon back into its holster.

Gildea stepped inside and glanced at the bodies. "So that's what the shooting was. Drew themselves a hand from a permanent cold deck. Never did like old Rustling Bob or Reese much."

The wiry Scout dug a hand beneath his coat and pulled out a single page of newspaper. "We got troubles, John."

"We haven't had anything but troubles for weeks. Why should it be any different now?"

Gildea handed the page of newsprint to John. "New governor's got some starch in his britches. Lew Wallace has just declared open season on us."

John scanned the article. Wallace had declared amnesty for those involved in the Lincoln County War—except for the hired guns from out of state. Those men had two choices. Leave New Mexico or be hunted down and killed.

John handed the page back to Gus and smiled. "What the hell. I was getting bored with New Mexico anyway."

Gus folded the paper and tucked it back into his pocket. "So's Jesse Evans, John Long, and Ace Carr. Ran into Evans over at the trading post. Said they were headed for the Texas Panhandle country."

"Texas is looking better all the time," John said.

"Thought so myself." Gus nodded toward the door. "Looks like a good time to load down a pack horse." He toed Rustling Bob Irwin's lifeless leg. "What do we do with these two?"

John shrugged. "Leave 'em lay. Come on, boys. Let's go home to Texas."

SIX

Fort Davis, Texas
August 1879

John Selman hitched the gold-heavy money belt more comfortably around his waist and watched the heat waves shimmer across the rugged, rocky hills north of the Big Bend country of West Texas. A few miles to the southwest lay the second Fort Davis John had known.

The Fort Davis of his earlier days was gone now, the rolling hills and rich grass of the Clear Fork of the Brazos only a memory. The present Fort Davis was the new edge of the frontier, standing watch over the main trails through the ragged canyons of the Big Bend into Mexico.

West Texas, from the boomtown of Tascosa on the distant plains of the Panhandle to the sun-baked settlement of Presidio on the Rio Grande, had been kind to John Selman and the Scouts. Horses, mules, and cattle were there for the taking, and buyers plentiful from Kansas all the way into Mexico. Homes, stores, isolated trading posts, and even freight wagons were an easy source of ready cash and supplies. As Tom Cat put it, "A man who can't make a good living here sure as hell isn't much of an outlaw."

John had even found the opportunity to provide for his children. Earlier in the year in Presidio County he had signed a power of attorney giving John C. McGrew, a relative of Edna's, authority to sell the Selman holdings on the Clear Fork and put the money to the care and education of the four children. Soon, he thought wistfully, he'd be able to send for them.

His scout of the countryside was complete. He had found two

remote canyons with enough water and grass to hold the horses stolen in a series of raids on ranches in the Staked Plains. He kneed his horse toward the gang's current headquarters on the banks of a spring-fed creek fifteen miles from Fort Davis. The headache that had ridden with him since dawn had worsened. It had started as a minor nuisance and built to a steady, grinding pain, as if a tent stake had been driven into one temple and out the other.

By the time he reached the lean-to shelter on the spring, John was shaking with chill despite the summer sun. The chill would pass, then a flush of heat would build until sweat poured from his body, only to trigger the next wave of shudders. *Must have gotten some bad water somewhere,* he told himself.

He left the horse saddled and stumbled into the shade of the lean-to. Every joint and muscle in his body hurt. The chills and fever came in stronger waves. The headache seemed to feed upon itself until John thought his head would explode like a melon blasted by a buffalo gun. He lowered himself onto the ground-sheet where his bedroll lay and groaned aloud in misery.

Tom Cat Selman rode into camp at sundown to find his brother twisting on his blankets, shivering and sweating.

Three days later a rash appeared on John Selman's body. By the fifth day, there was no question in Tom Selman's mind about what John's ailment was.

Tom had seen smallpox before.

A short, ugly Comanche squaw cackled in glee as she slapped the prickly pear against John's legs. Then she crept away, leaving him to the agony. Other figures took her place—a stocky Scot and five hazy forms pointing cocked pistols at John's head. John braced himself for the bullet, but it never came. The gunmen dissolved, melted away on a red mist. John was in the saddle, riding along a tree-lined creek. He tried to scream at the sight of four small bodies—his children—dangling by the neck on ropes from a tall tree, just beyond reach, and he could only watch as tiny feet kicked out the last spark of life. He felt the tears on his face and turned to Edna. Her body was covered in blood, with only the whites of accusing eyes visible, staring at him. John heard, from a distance, his own choked sob as the darkness reached for him. He tried to grasp it, pull it to him, escape from the horror, but he couldn't reach its comfort. Then he was in a casket of glass, unable to scream or speak, looking up at a sky the color of brass. He saw the shovelful of dirt fall toward his face, thump against the glass, cover part of the sky. He heard the muted voice of the Reverend C. C. Slaughter reciting the opening words of the 23rd Psalm. Then the earth covered the glass of his coffin. The darkness was complete.

The figure was there again, but this time there was less form to the edges, and it wasn't a Comanche squaw.

"Who—who's there?" John's voice was a croak.

"Easy, *señor.*" The voice was soft, soothing. "I am Guadalupe Zarate. This"—the figure gestured toward the hazy form of a slender young woman—"is my daughter, Niconora."

"What—how—"

"Be quiet, *señor.* Rest. I will tell you how this came to be. Niconora and I were traveling in our wagon when we saw the buzzards on the top of your tent. We found you here, near death, suffering terrible dreams. We washed you and nursed you. I think now you will live, but you will bear the scars of the pox forever."

John sagged back on the makeshift cot, exhausted. For the first time in what seemed to be years, there was little pain. Memories returned in flashes and fragments. How Tom Cat and Ace Carr had propped him in the saddle, brought him to Fort Davis. Put up the tent a half mile outside of town, hired someone to watch over him. Someone named Gotch.

"Where's—Gotch?"

Zarate shrugged. "I do not know of this man. You were alone here. It has been a week now. I do not think this Gotch is nearby."

The bastard, John thought, *I remember now; he left to go get a bottle of whiskey and never came back.* The darkness came once more, this time without the spectre of the grave. John Selman slept. There were no dreams.

John's recovery was rapid once the crisis had passed. He came to admire the simple Mexican tailor and the serene young woman who prayed over him each day, tended his dressings, and fed him until he was strong enough to care for himself.

He had also come to realize that Niconora Zarate was a special woman, educated, kind, and considerate. A devout Catholic, attractive by any man's standards, with a soft and soothing voice. Expressive dark brown eyes framed by hair the color of a raven's wing. The kind of woman men would kill for. The kind they would never forget. The kind of woman who could help ease a man's earlier loss.

Guadalupe Zarate was a man of honor and compassion. Zarate accepted without censure that the man whose life he had saved had killed and stolen. "Each man walks his own path," Zarate said with a gentle smile. "It is not my place to judge him. Only God has that power."

By the end of the third week, the disease had run its course. John's strength grew by the day, the scabs of the pustules mending into scars. He was now capable of caring for his own needs, and he knew that he had stalled Guadalupe Zarate's plans to open his tailor shop long enough.

As the Zarates loaded their wagon for the short trip into Fort Davis, John offered Guadalupe two hundred dollars from the gold in his money belt. The tailor shook his head.

"I am not a rich man, *Señor* Selman, nor am I poor. I will not accept money for anything Niconora or I have done here. It is enough that you live. It is enough that you remember us in fondness and friendship. That is a thing that gold cannot buy."

John stood before the tent and watched Zarate's wagon pull away. Niconora turned and waved. *Fondness and friendship,* John thought as he returned the salute. In the woman's case, he admitted, a feeling that had grown stronger than friendship. He would miss her smile, her touch, the comfortable feeling of just being in her presence.

But not for long.

John Selman wandered back into the tent that had been his home and his hospital for a month. It seemed even more empty than it was. He shook the vision of Niconora from his mind. There were plans to be made.

Fort Davis, Texas
May 1880

Sergeant L. B. Caruthers of the Texas Rangers leaned against the hitch-rail of a general store across the street from Captain John Tyson's butcher shop, brow furrowed in thought.

There was something about the man who called himself John Tyson that drew the ranger back time and again to watch the butcher shop. Caruthers had other things to do; Fort Davis and neighboring Fort Stockton were lawless, wide-open towns, the merchants and townspeople in constant fear of robbery or worse. And since Tyson had opened his business earlier in the year, the raids had become more frequent. The outlaws who camped in the surrounding hills seemed to know exactly when to strike, when a business would have the most money on hand. Someone in Fort Davis was feeding them information. Caruthers had an inkling of who that someone was.

The butcher-shop door was open to the mild spring breeze. Caruthers watched as two Mexican women emerged carrying parcels. The sergeant knew the women to be from poverty-stricken homes. He also knew that the man named Tyson seldom charged the poorest Mexicans for scraps of meat. There was very little solid information on Tyson to be had from the Mexican community of Fort Davis. He was *amigo* to many, *patrón* to a few, and was a frequent visitor to the tailor shop owned by Guadalupe Zarate. There was a rumor that he and Niconora Zarate were planning to be married.

Tyson came to the door, wiping his hands on a smudged apron. The man looked familiar, somehow, to Caruthers. The sergeant would have bet a month's pay that Tyson was not the butcher's real name. Everybody in this godforsaken country had an alias or two, it seemed. Caruthers studied Tyson again, as if seeing him for the first time. Five-ten, solid build, maybe a hundred sixty pounds. Gray hair and eyes of pale blue. His face was heavily scarred and pitted, beardless, but with a full mustache. He walked with a downcast look, spoke Spanish and a couple of Indian dialects. And he was never without a handgun, either beneath his apron or on his hip.

Caruthers couldn't shake the feeling that this was a dangerous man. The ranger had learned to trust his instincts. Tyson—or whatever his name was—would bear watching . . .

John Selman, now known as Captain John Tyson, formerly of the Confederate Army, squatted in front of the smoky campfire in the mountain hideout across from Jesse Evans, dragged on his pipe, and relaxed after the ride from his home in Fort Davis. Few of the original Scouts had remained loyal to Selman in the days of his illness, and he felt a special warmth toward those few who had— Evans, Tom Cat, Ace Carr, John Gross, and Charlie Graves in particular. Most of the others had struck out on their own.

"I think I've got a good one for us this time, Jesse," Selman said. "Sender and Seibenborn just closed a big sale in Mexico and another with the Butterfield freight people. Their store will be running over with cash money at the end of the week."

Evans squinted through the campfire smoke and grinned. "Should be easy enough to relieve a couple of Fort Davis's leading merchants of their profits. How much you reckon there'll be?"

"No way to know for sure. Close to a thousand, probably."

"Damn, this is better than owning a bank," Evans said. "How you want to set it up, John?"

Less than an hour later, John Selman was in the saddle, heading home to Fort Davis. Maybe the pox had been a blessing in disguise; scarred as his face was, nobody in Fort Davis would be able to recognize him as Selman. The butcher shop, with its back room for living quarters, was a perfect front to keep track of where the money was. It even showed a decent profit on its own. All he had to do was funnel information to Evans and the boys in the hideout north of town, and collect his share of the take.

Best of all, the shop let him be close to Niconora most of the time. They had already agreed on the date for the wedding—June 26, 1880.

After that day, John would be a happily married man, retired from the outlaw trade with a hefty nest egg and a growing business that wasn't likely to get a man shot or hanged.

• • • •

Jesse Evans and the boys made a quick, clean cut on Sender and
Siebenborn's store.

With Gross acting as a lookout, Jesse, Tom Cat, and Ace Carr
walked into the store, pulled handguns, trussed up everyone
inside, and walked away with the cash. Four hundred silver dollars, two hundred in Mexican coin, and another two hundred in
American greenbacks. No one was hurt, and the raiders were well
on their way back into the wild and rugged Davis Mountains
before the call for help was sounded.

Sergeant Caruthers returned to Fort Davis three days after the
robbery, butt-sore and dead tired. The trail had led into the
mountains and promptly vanished. As he rode his exhausted
mount back into Fort Davis, Caruthers turned in the saddle and
stared toward Tyson's butcher shop.

The hunt had not been a complete failure. At an abandoned
outlaw camp, Caruthers had cut sign on a horse with a peculiar
half-moon chip knocked from the shoe on the left forefoot.

Caruthers knew that track. It belonged to John Tyson's sorrel
gelding. Caruthers also had a witness able to name two of the
men in the robbery. Jesse Evans and Ace Carr. Known friends of
the man called John Selman. *Enjoy your freedom while you can, Selman,* Caruthers silently vowed. *All I need is one mistake and I'll have
your hide on the wall.*

Fort Davis
June 1880

John Selman slammed his butcher knife into the chopping block
with enough force to bury the sharp point a half inch into the
hard wood.

Of all the damn fool things Ace Carr could have done, this one
cut the devil's tail to the bone. Ace had ignored the number one
rule of survival as an outlaw. He had spent the money too close to
where it came from.

With the Sender and Seibenborn money scorching their pockets, Carr, Jesse Evans, and Charlie Graves had decided to tree the

town in Fort Stockton. An armed mob of angry citizens decided they didn't want the town treed, and Carr was foolish enough—or drunk enough—to get himself caught.

If it weren't so damn serious, Selman thought, it would be downright comical. Now that the townspeople had Carr, they were afraid *they* had made the mistake. Evans, Graves, and the others were in the mountains, and Fort Stockton was almost on its knees in fear the outlaws would slash into the town at any minute, free Carr, and burn the community for its impudence.

The rangers were in a bind, too. Having to guard Carr around the clock meant they didn't have enough men left to hunt for the others. In a way, Selman could sympathize with Caruthers, who was an occasional customer in John's shop. The Fort Davis sheriff, a man named Wilson who had a penchant for the bottle, was no help. Neither the citizens of Fort Davis nor those of Fort Stockton would support the rangers for fear of retaliation. Caruthers was between the devil and the Pecos River, with no trail out. It would be interesting to see how the young sergeant handled this herd.

A commotion out on the street drew John's attention. He stepped to the door as the procession passed. Ace Carr rode with head bowed, shoulders slumped, and hands bound, amid an escort of four rangers. There was no mistaking their destination: the underground jail known as the "bat cave" beneath the courthouse. That jail, John knew, would be a hell of a lot harder to take than the adobe lockup in Fort Stockton.

Hang on a while, Ace, John vowed silently. *The boys and I will figure a way to get you out.*

Ranger Sergeant L. B. Caruthers eased his aching body into the chair behind the sheriff's desk. As usual, when danger was about, Sheriff Wilson was nowhere to be seen.

The jailor, too, was gone. The door had barely banged shut over Ace Carr's "cell" before he had resigned, afraid of catching some lead when Carr's outlaw friends came to wreck the place. Caruthers didn't worry about that much. The man wasn't to be trusted, anyway.

The sergeant propped his feet on the desk and leaned back in the chair. He had Carr in custody in a relatively secure jail. That would free several rangers to concentrate on the other outlaws. But that didn't solve the matter of John Selman, alias Captain John Tyson. Still, Caruthers told himself, a thinking man could turn almost any situation to his own advantage. The seed of a plan took root in the ranger's mind. Within the hour it had grown to full bloom.

John Selman glanced up as Caruthers strode into the butcher shop. John's hand drifted to the pistol beneath his apron, but he made no effort to draw the weapon. There was no threat in the ranger's expression, only a casual nod of greeting.

"Captain Tyson, I need a favor," Caruthers said. "The jailor has quit us. Afraid of Carr's friends, it appears. That leaves us short of help, and we need a man with proven leadership ability and courage. A man like yourself, who commanded men in battle."

Selman let his hand fall away from his waistband. "What do you have in mind, Sergeant?"

"I know it's asking a lot, your being married just a couple of days ago." Caruthers let a note of apology creep into his words. "But I'd like to ask you to take over as night jailor and deputy, until this business with Ace Carr is finished. If you can see your way clear to leave your business here for a few days, it would be a great service to the rangers—and to the people of Fort Davis."

John blinked in disbelief. Here was a ranger sergeant offering him the one post where he could best help his friend escape. It was clear proof that Caruthers had no idea who he really was, and that the law had never connected him with the robberies in Fort Davis. John smiled at Caruthers. "I would be glad to do my civic duty, Sergeant," he said. "I'll get a friend to mind the butcher shop. When do I report?"

"This evening, after supper, would be best—if it isn't too short notice," Caruthers said. "My personal thanks, Captain Tyson. You will be paid for your services, of course. Please express my regards to your new wife, a lovely woman."

Caruthers offered his hand, then turned and stepped into the heat of the noon sun. *By God, he bought it,* the ranger thought. *That will keep him where we can watch him until we spring the trap on the others.* Caruthers fingered the faded paper in his pocket. It was an old warrant from Shackleford County, found in a cluttered drawer of Wilson's desk.

Caruthers could have arrested Selman on the spot, but this way he solved several problems. The rangers had no solid proof that Selman was the leader of the gang. Not enough to take to court. As jailor, Selman might make a mistake, or at least he could be watched until someone talked. He would not be able to communicate with the other outlaws in the hills. And in the end, it was more important to rid the country of the whole gang than simply to hold two men.

Now word would be leaked to Selman's bunch that the rangers were moving out on patrol, leaving Selman to guard Ace Carr. It was the kind of bait the gang couldn't resist. When they bit, and rode into Fort Davis to free Carr, there would be Texas Rangers in every building around the jail, all armed with shotguns and rifles.

Caruthers squared his shoulders and strode down the street toward the courthouse. In a matter of days, West Texas would be free of Selman's Scouts. Ranger Sergeant Caruthers was not an ambitious man, but he wouldn't object in the least to the lieutenant's rank and pay raise that was sure to come to the man who broke the back of the Selman gang.

An insistent pounding on the door of his rented room dragged Caruthers from a deep sleep. The clock on the fireplace mantel read four in the morning. Caruthers wiped a hand across his scratchy eyes and opened the door.

Ranger Red Bingham wasted no time with idle greetings. "Sergeant, we've got troubles. Somehow, Sheriff Wilson found out about our plan. He got into a tussle with a bottle and started talking. Now the whole county will know what we're up to. I wouldn't be surprised if somebody isn't in the saddle right now to warn Selman's boys."

Caruthers sighed. "Well, Red, it looks like we have to do it the hard way now." He spoke as he dressed, strapped on his gunbelt, and reached for his hat. "I'll get Selman out of the way. Get Sergeant Seiker and any other rangers you can find into the saddle. We'll have to just dig the outlaws out, now. And if anybody can find a reason to pistol-whip that damned Wilson, I would consider it a personal favor."

Caruthers knocked on the door of the courthouse and waited until John Selman opened the door. He pulled his pistol and stepped inside.

"What is this, Sergeant?" Selman's gaze moved from the muzzle of Caruthers's handgun to the ranger's face in confusion.

"John Selman, I'm placing you under arrest on an indictment for cattle theft from Shackleford County. Now, ease that gun out of the holster. Left hand, thumb, and little finger. Put it on the desk."

Selman had no choice but to do as he was told.

Moments later the trap door opened over Ace Carr's head and John Selman dropped through into the "bat cave."

"John! What are you doing down here? Are the others here already?"

"No, dammit." John Selman spat. "I'm your bunkmate for a spell. Hell of a way for a man to spend his honeymoon, isn't it?"

Fort Davis
July 1880

John Selman slouched on one end of the low cot that served as his bunk in the gloomy cell and flipped a tattered card toward Ace Carr. Neither man was particularly interested in poker with no money involved, but it passed the time.

Ace tried a grin. "Could be worse," he said. "At least it's cool down here. Been in lockups that were hotter than—" A clatter of boots on the floor above cut Carr short.

Jesse Evans was the first one into the cell, with John Gross and Charlie Graves close behind. The trap door slammed shut.

Evans grunted a greeting to John and Carr. "Never thought I'd actually be glad to see the inside of a jail," Evans said with a wry grin. "I wasn't sure until just now that those rangers weren't going to lynch us."

John pulled his pipe from a pocket, forgetting he was out of tobacco. "What happened, Jesse?"

Evans brushed a cobweb aside and leaned against the damp wall. "These rangers are damn good at their job, John. Tracked us for days. Jumped us on the way to the hideout in the Chinatis. Bud Graham got shot in the head. We killed one of the rangers. They had us pinned down on a rocky hill. We had to give up or get picked off one at a time."

Evans paused and took a deep breath. "Those rangers would have killed us right then, but they didn't find out for a while that the one we shot was dead. I tell you, if we had so much as sneezed on the way in they'd have put a pound of lead in each of us."

"What about Tom?"

Evans slid down the wall into a sitting position. "Tom Cat wasn't with us. When we turned north toward the mountains, he headed east. Don't know if anybody cut his trail or not."

John glanced around the now-crowded cell. *It's over,* he told himself, *Selman's Scouts have nothing left but a rope or prison.* At least he knew Niconora wouldn't be in need. He had left all but a few dollars of his considerable stash in her care. *I'm sorry, Niconora. I'd hoped for more than this for us.*

Griffin, Texas

Shackleford County Sheriff William Cruger read the message from Fort Davis a second time, cursing each word on the telegram. The rangers were sending John Selman to Shackleford County to stand trial on warrants dating back two years.

Cruger tossed the telegram to Bill Hawsley, seated across the desk.

"Dammit, Bill," Cruger said, "we can't take Selman to trial here. If he gets on the stand and starts talking—" He didn't have to finish the statement. Bill Hawsley knew how many prominent names would be dragged down by the aging gunman's testimony.

"So what do we do, Sheriff? Kill him?"

"Not worth the risk. Selman still has friends all over the country. They'd tree this town and Albany both. Our lives wouldn't be worth a Confederate dollar." Cruger paused to roll and light a cigarette, then exhaled toward the ceiling. "I've done everything

I can to convince the rangers we don't want Selman. They're not buying it. So there's just one thing we can do, Bill. Turn Selman loose."

Albany, Texas
August 1880

John Selman sat on the edge of his bunk in the Albany jail, manacled hands clenched into fists.

"I'm sorry about Tom," Sheriff Bill Cruger said.

Selman half believed the sheriff meant it. He fixed a cold stare on Cruger's face and held it until the sheriff's gaze fell. "You have anything to do with that, Cruger?"

"No, John. I swear to you. I wasn't even in Comanche when the —when it happened."

"Go ahead and say it, Cruger. When a mob pulled him from a jail cell and lynched him like a common horse thief." John knew Cruger was telling the truth—the man was a terrible liar—and that was the only thing that kept him from jumping the sheriff and squeezing the life from his throat.

Tom Cat Selman had deserved a better end. That he had not been there to help his brother left a bitter taste in the back of John Selman's throat. The certainty that he would have been hanged along with Tom did nothing to ease his pain.

Cruger cleared his throat. "John, there are a number of us around Albany who think you got a deal from a stacked deck. If we hold you here for trial, somebody's likely to try the same thing with you they did with your brother. We've got a proposition."

"Which is?"

"Sundown tonight, we give you a horse. You give us your word you'll never set foot in Shackleford County again."

John Selman dropped his gaze to the chain between his ankles, studying his options. He was sure there wasn't enough evidence or witnesses to convict him in court. He wasn't at all sure he wouldn't be shot by Cruger "while trying to escape." He was reasonably sure that if he stayed in Albany he'd be yanked from jail and lynched. He was positive about only one thing. The long days in the cell in Fort Davis had convinced him that anything was better than being locked up.

There was nothing he could do for Tom. Even revenge was beyond his reach. The men who broke the Comanche jail and lynched Tom were all masked. Given time, John might be able to find out who they were.

But he didn't have the luxury of time. If Cruger was playing it straight with him, there was still Niconora and a new life in Mexico. If he wasn't, a quick bullet was a better way to go than a noose.

John looked up at Cruger.

"Agreed," he said.

SEVEN

San Pablo, Mexico
Spring 1881

John Selman stood on the platform of the railway station, his arm around Niconora's waist, and squinted toward the north where a smudge of smoke from the El Paso train blotched the horizon.

Two of his children were coming home.

He glanced at his wife's face. The smooth jawline was tense, and small crow's feet crinkled the corners of her eyes.

"Nervous, Niconora?" He gave her waist a reassuring squeeze.

"Yes, John. What if they do not like me?"

John chuckled. "Niconora, there is no way they could help but like you." He forced a mock frown onto his face. "If they do not, I will send them back—because someone will have sent me the wrong children."

The comment brought a smile from Niconora. John knew how she felt. He was a bit concerned himself. It had been a long time since he had seen William and John Junior. The worry was clouded by a lingering touch of hurt. Henry, his firstborn, and Margaretta had chosen to stay with the McGrew family on the ranch near old Fort Griffin. The rejection pained John Selman more than any rifle bullet could.

John pulled Niconora closer as the train neared San Pablo. Such a public display would be a scandal north of the border, he mused, but the Mexicans viewed it as the expression of tenderness that it was meant to be. This was one of the reasons John felt such a warmth toward the land and its people. They weren't afraid to show affection. He wished he had learned how to show it better himself.

The locomotive pulled into the San Pablo station belching steam, ash, and dense smoke. John's palm was wet. He let his hand drop from Niconora's waist before the sweat stained her dress.

Six-year-old John Junior was in his father's arms moments after his feet touched Mexican soil. William offered a solemn handshake, man to man, as befitted his advanced age of eleven.

"Niconora, I'd like you to meet my sons," John said after the greetings. "This," he rumpled his youngest son's hair, "is John Selman, Junior. The other gentleman is William, better known now as Bud. Boys, meet your new mother, Niconora Zarate Selman."

Any fears Niconora had about John's sons were soon allayed. By the time the boys' bags—one small case each—had been located, the initial shyness was gone. John Junior, the demonstrative one, now held Niconora's hand. Bud, more reserved by nature and feeling the importance of his years, offered a hand to help Niconora into the buggy that waited just beyond the station house.

"Well, boys," John Selman said as he clucked the buggy horse into motion, "welcome to San Pablo and home. We've a nice place on the edge of town. You'll each have your own room."

"Dad, is it a farm?" Bud's question held a note of apprehension.

"No, son. It isn't a farm."

"Good. I hate farms."

John glanced over his shoulder at his son. "Why do you say that, Bud?"

The youth held up his hands. The palms were calloused, fingernails chipped and ragged. "Mister McGrew, he made us kids work on his neighbors' farms, and he kept the money."

John Selman bit back a curse. "What else did Mister McGrew do?"

Bud was silent for a moment, as though choosing his words with care. "He told Henry he couldn't come with us. Said he needed him too much. And Missus McGrew told Margaretta you didn't want her. Is that true, Dad?"

John's anger flared. "No, Bud. It's not true at all! And if I ever get my hands on McGrew—" He didn't finish the sentence.

• • • •

The days passed quickly for John Selman. San Pablo was a good place to live. The cantina he had been operating since he and Niconora arrived continued to turn a nice profit. The kids had taken to Niconora like puppies to warm biscuits, just as John had expected. After a few days the boys were calling her "Mother" without any discomfort. Bud even overcame his loathing for farming enough to help Niconora in the garden.

John Junior picked up Spanish with a speed that astonished even his father. Soon he could swear with the fluency of a horse wrangler. John had to scold him once for using such language in front of his mother.

For the first time in years, John Selman began to feel he had a home once more.

San Pablo, Mexico
Summer 1883

Smallpox came swift and hard to San Pablo.

John Selman sold the cantina and came home to help within hours after the first ominous blotches appeared on young Bud's body. A day later they appeared on John Junior's.

Day and night seemed to run together for John and Niconora, an endless series of warm baths of diluted carbolic, cleansing the pustules, trying to get some nourishment into the small, tormented bodies.

From his own experience John knew what the children were going through, the muscle pains, the infuriating agony of the constant itching.

Every day seemed to bring more funeral processions along the road past the Selman home to the San Pablo cemetery. It seemed to John that two of every three coffins were less than four feet long, carried on the sorrowed shoulders of a father with a weeping mother following close behind.

John alternately prayed and cursed. He prayed for the Creator to spare his children. He cursed the disease, battled it, stood at the doorway while the funerals passed as if he could keep death from his home by sheer brute force. He tried to funnel his own strength to the two small forms in the back room. And to Nico-nora. John knew the strain of worry and around-the-clock nursing had taken its toll on her. She never complained, but exhaustion drew its lines across the smooth skin of her face, and pushed heavily on her shoulders.

On the morning of the fifteenth day since young Bud had awakened complaining of a headache and fever, John sat slouched and half dozing at the table, a forgotten cup of coffee growing cold before him.

He straightened at the touch of Niconora's hand. "The danger is past, John," Niconora said. "They will live. Bud will bear the scars. I do not think John Junior will be badly marked, if at all."

John placed his own hand over Niconora's and leaned his head against her. "God has blessed this house, Niconora. And me in particular. He brought you to save first my own life, then that of the boys." He looked up at her and swallowed against the lump in his throat. "You're a good woman, Niconora. More than I deserve. I don't know what I would do without you."

Niconora brushed her lips against his forehead. "And you are a good man, John Selman. Would you like some breakfast?"

"I would like, Niconora Zarate Selman, for you to go straight to bed and sleep for a week. You've more than earned it, girl."

John Selman tugged the final knot into place on the mule pack and patted the animal's neck. The mule returned the gesture by trying to take a nip from John's hip. John retaliated with a solid slap to the side of the animal's nose. It was a routine they had gone through every week for months now, the dispute over who was going to be the boss for the forty-mile trip to San Pablo.

The silver mine John had claimed, after the threat of smallpox had passed, had fed his family well. Now, the bags were lighter with each trip; the vein was playing out. It was only a matter of time until he would have to support his family by other means.

Before starting the long ride home, John paid the three Mexicans who helped work the mine. It was his way of assuring them that their families would not go hungry if something should happen to him during the trip. There were always bandits about in the hills of Mexico. John didn't worry about them much. As he had told his workers, if he spent his time fretting over every campfire yarn in these dry mountains, he wouldn't have time to piss, let alone dig silver.

Still, he checked the loads in the Colt and the Winchester before stepping into the saddle.

As he rode, John let his mind drift back through the years and the men he had ridden with. There were few of them left. From the Tonkawa Indian, Whiskey Pete, to John Larn to Billy Bland to Tom Cat Selman, a string of deaths by gunshot or lynch rope. John Long was believed to have been killed in a botched holdup in West Texas.

Jesse Evans had escaped from the Huntsville prison and disappeared. John half expected Jesse to appear from behind a brush clump at any moment. John Gross was still in the Texas lockup, serving ten years for attempted murder. Of Ace Carr and Gus Gildea nothing was known.

Many of those John Selman had ridden against were dead too, including Billy the Kid—shot by Pat Garrett the year John and Niconora had fled to Mexico. In the Anglo newspapers that sometimes surfaced in San Pablo, John read that Wyatt Earp and Doc Holliday, his one-time poker companions in Griffin, had bloodied the Clanton gang in a place called the OK Corral in Tombstone. John Wesley Hardin, who had left his calling card tacked to a post in a Griffin saloon, was serving fifteen years for killing the deputy sheriff of Comanche.

The days of the gunman were numbered, it seemed.

A movement a quarter mile up the trail stopped the tumble of names through John's head.

Two riders in broad-brimmed Mexican hats and serapes rode from the brush onto the trail. John cocked the Winchester by instinct, but soon relaxed as he recognized the horsemen—Joaquin Estrada and his mute brother, Cesar.

Estrada, the *segundo* of a sprawling *ranchero* a few miles south of San Pablo, raised a hand in greeting. John lowered the hammer of the rifle and slipped it into the saddle boot.

"Greetings, John Selman," Estrada said. "How goes the silver mine?"

"It is like a woman past her prime, Joaquin. And the ranch?"

Estrada smiled, a flash of white teeth against swarthy skin. "A woman just beginning to bloom, John." The smile faded. "Have you seen any horse tracks? We seem to be missing a few."

John shook his head. "Nothing between here and the mine, Joaquin. Thieves?"

Estrada shrugged. "This I do not know. Perhaps only strayed. I will find out." The ranch foreman's tone held no outward menace, but John knew that if rustlers were involved, their days left on this earth were now few. Joaquin Estrada was not a man to steal from if one expected a long career. Cesar was just as dangerous. John had at first wondered why the man never spoke. Then one day he had noticed the puckered scar at the side of the stocky Cesar's throat. It was obvious he had been rendered mute by a bullet.

John quelled a sudden urge to ride along with the Estradas. It had been a long time since he had been on the trail, and the company of good men on the hunt had always been a tonic. But then, he reminded himself, no man could find a better tonic than a family and a good woman. He touched the brim of his hat. "Good hunting, Joaquin."

The tall Mexican smiled and nodded. "John, when you tire of digging in the dirt like a peon, come and work with me. I need a man who knows good horses."

"*Gracias*, Joaquin. I will keep that in mind."

"*Vaya con Dios*, John Selman." Joaquin reined his bay toward the northwest.

"*Vaya con Dios*, Joaquin."

John watched until the two horsemen disappeared into the distance, then kneed his own mount toward home.

San Pablo, Mexico
Winter 1886

John Selman awoke to the predawn darkness and listened to the wind murmur against the adobe walls. The Texas Plains far to the north would be bitterly cold today, he thought. February northers seldom drove this far into Mexico, and the temperature outside would be well above freezing, but John knew the people of San Pablo were not accustomed to even a slight chill.

Uneasiness edged along John's spine. It was quiet in the bedroom. Too quiet. Twice during the night he had awakened at the sound of Niconora's shallow, labored breathing, the rattling cough. Now there was no sound from the still figure at his side.

John reached out to Niconora, put his palm against her cheek. The skin was cool to the touch. He dropped his hand to her chest. There was no movement, no heartbeat.

Fear gave way to a crushing emptiness in John Selman's heart. He lowered his head to the still breast.

The gray light of dawn filtered through the west bedroom window before John Selman stirred. He wiped the tears from his cheeks and tucked the blankets around Niconora's shoulders, his touch tender.

John squared his shoulders against the weight of grief and strode into the adjoining bedroom. He stood for a moment above the small forms huddled beneath the blankets, listened to the soft buzz of Bud's snore. Then he shook the two boys awake.

"What is it, Dad?" John Junior rubbed a knuckle against sleepy eyes.

"It's your mother, son," John said softly. "She's dead."

Almost all of San Pablo came to pay their respects to Niconora Selman. John greeted them in a daze, as if he were someone else watching the proceedings. Wealthy ranchers stood side by side with peons as the casket was lowered into the stark grave in the San Pablo cemetery.

Joaquin and Cesar Estrada stood near John, hats in hand. Tears of sorrow welled in the mute's eyes. Niconora and John had become special favorites of the Estrada brothers after the silver mine played out and John went to work with them on the ranch. That was more than a year ago.

John barely heard the chant of the priest, but watched in detached disbelief as the casket laden with paper flowers was lowered into the earth.

He stood unmoving as the grave was filled. A touch on his shoulder brought him back to the stark reality of the moment.

"*Señor* John, I will watch over the boys for a while," a wrinkled woman in a threadbare shawl said. "You may stay with her as long as you wish. Perhaps it will ease the pain of your loss."

"Thank you, Marietta."

The woman led John Junior and Bud away, a comforting arm on the shoulders of each small body. The remainder of the funeral party began to trickle away.

The high gray clouds broke during the late afternoon. The westering sun painted a soft gold over the mound of fresh dirt, and still John Selman stood at Niconora's grave.

At length, John became aware of a presence at his side. He turned to Joaquin Estrada and saw a reflection of his own pain in the ranch foreman's eyes.

"Has it not been long enough, my friend?" Joaquin's words were soft, gentle.

John turned his gaze back to the grave. "I never knew a man could hurt so much, Joaquin," he said. "And the thing that cuts the deepest is that I don't remember the last time I told her I loved her."

"She knew, John Selman. Now it is time for you to try to survive. You have two young sons depending upon you. You have many friends who will help when needed or asked."

John choked back his pain. "When my first wife died, Joaquin, I was able to ease the hurt with vengeance, by killing the man responsible for her death. But how does a man gain revenge against lung fever?"

Joaquin shrugged and reached into a vest pocket. "One cannot, John. It leaves an empty anger in the heart not to be able to strike back." He handed a flask to John. "You will always have Niconora in your heart. Life does not end for the living. That is perhaps the cruelest thing about the death of a loved one."

John lifted the flask and downed two swallows of tequila. The raw liquor settled its warmth in his stomach. He twisted the cap back onto the flask and returned it to Joaquin.

"What will you do now, John?"

John was silent for several heartbeats. "I don't know, Joaquin. There isn't much left for me in San Pablo with Niconora gone. I've heard of a gold strike in the Mogollon Mountains in New Mexico. Maybe I'll check it out."

"Sometimes it is best that a man leave a place of hurt for a little while. To give the heart time to mend." Joaquin put a hand on John's shoulder. "Your friends here will see that John Junior and Bud are never alone or in need while you are away. When you return from your quest, your job will still be waiting at our ranch."

San Pablo, Mexico
April 1888

John Selman sat in Niconora's rocking chair and sucked at a drop of blood from a fingertip stabbed by a slip of the sewing needle. "Dammit, Niconora," he cursed as though she sat with him, "I never was able to get the hang of this."

He turned his attention back to the hole he was attempting to mend in the elbow of Bud's shirt. It seemed the kids were in some kind of a race to see which one could outgrow or wear out clothes the quickest. In better times he would have given the shirt to a peasant family and bought a new one. But the rumor of gold in the Mogollons had been just that—a rumor.

John had returned home almost broke, but the solitude of the mountain wilderness had healed some of the pain in his heart. He could face a new day now without the bitterness and anger, the nagging sense of helplessness that had dogged him for months after Niconora's death.

He examined his handiwork on the shirt and found it wanting, but at least it would hold together. He tossed it aside as Bud bustled through the door, an envelope in his hand.

"Letter, Dad," Bud said. "All the way from Albany. From Uncle Jasper."

John slit the envelope with his pocketknife. Letters from Jasper deGraffenreid were rare but welcome, a tenuous touch with the green and rolling hills of the Clear Fork country.

He scanned the letter and felt a smile spread across his face as he went back to the first line and read each word with care. Then he tucked it into a shirt pocket.

"Bud, find John Junior for me. It's good news for once. The

Thirty-fourth District Court in Albany has dismissed all the charges against me. We're going home, son. Home to Texas."

A short time later, John knelt at the grave of Niconora Zarate Selman. He plucked a couple of weeds from among the tender green blades of grass on the low mound.

"Well, Niconora," John said, a mix of joy and sorrow in his voice, "I suppose I'll be leaving you again. But you'll always be with me in my memories. And I'll come back as often as I can to visit . . ."

EIGHT

El Paso, Texas
Summer 1888

John Selman's return to Texas stopped just north of the Rio Grande.

A day in El Paso was enough to convince John that he belonged. The place was a boomtown, the original squat and ugly adobe buildings rapidly giving way to two- and three-story frame structures. The railroads had triggered the explosive growth of El Paso, and transformed the sleepy little village of five hundred into a city of almost ten thousand residents in less than a decade.

It wasn't the prosperous economy of El Paso that gripped and held John Selman. It was the feel of the place. The faces were different, the buildings taller, the air drier, and the mountains always in sight. But the character of El Paso was almost a mirror of the Fort Griffin country John had loved—a brawling, whiskey-drinking, gambling, whoring place where a man's past meant little.

John Selman knew immediately that El Paso was his kind of town.

Within a week he had bought a house on Santa Fe Street in lower El Paso and found work.

The streets of El Paso teemed with heavily armed and hard-eyed men on both sides of the law, but John's own reputation with a gun had preceded him. At first the stares, whispers, and occasional fingers pointed in his direction bothered him. He soon learned to ignore the unwanted attention.

He stood at the bar of the Red Light Saloon on Utah Street, washing the day's labor from his throat and idly passing the time with Jim Burns, the owner of the establishment, when a young man in a bowler hat and silk suit stepped up beside him.

"Mister Selman? John Selman?"

John glanced at the youthful face, tinged pink by sun and wind. A speckling of El Paso dust grayed the black bowler hat. "Who wants to know?"

"My name's Hanratty, Mister Selman. Correspondent with the *Boston Globe*. I'm doing a series of stories on famous gunfighters of the West, sir. It's quite popular with our readers back East." Hanratty slipped a notebook and pencil from a breast pocket. "I'd like to tell your story, Mister Selman."

John sighed. "Mister Hanratty, somebody sold you a wind-broke horse."

"Beg pardon?"

"Wind-broke horse. Something next to worthless. Do you think a famous gunfighter would be working as a dump boss for a smelting plant? I'm just an old man trying to make a living."

"But sir, I was told—"

"You can hear anything in these whiskey mills, son." John sneaked a wink in Jim Burns's direction. The saloon owner was watching the exchange with interest. "I'll tell you what, Mister Hanratty. You see that man over there, at the corner table, with his back to the wall? The one in the blue shirt?"

The reporter nodded.

"Well, son. That man just happens to be Billy the Kid." John heard Jim Burns cough to cover a laugh. "Now, there's a story for you. Billy's from New York, you know. I bet your readers would eat that story up like a buttered biscuit."

The reporter cocked a cautious eyebrow at John. "I thought Billy the Kid was killed by Pat Garrett back in eighty-one."

John shrugged. "That was the story put out. Those who know the Kid say otherwise. That the Kid just got tired of running from the law, and he and Garrett staged the whole thing to take the heat off. That man over there knows things only the Kid would know."

The reporter's skepticism dissolved into eagerness. "Billy the Kid? Now that would be a story. Excuse me, sir, and thanks for your help."

John watched the young man hurry toward the table, then turned to Jim Burns. The saloon owner was chuckling aloud.

"I swear, John, if you ain't the bull that broke the fence." Burns shook his head. "Billy the Kid. You know damn well the closest that man ever came to a pistol was when he stole one and traded it for a bottle."

John grinned and waved for a refill. "Well, Jim, the kid with the pencil doesn't know that. I doubt the people in Boston know it. Everybody east of the Mississippi is claiming to be the Kid these days. So the reporter gets a story and leaves me alone. Hell, I've spent my whole life trying to keep my name *out* of the papers. This gives Smokey Willis a chance to be another famous gunfighter and talk the kid out of a bottle to boot. Everybody's happy."

Jim Burns filled John's glass and waved off the coin offered in payment. "Stunt like that's worth a drink on the Red Light anytime." Burns stared toward the corner table where young Hanratty was scribbling in his notebook as rapidly as he could. It wasn't hard to get Smokey to talk. It was hell's own wildfire to get him to stop.

"John, can I ask you something personal?"

"Ask away. Can't promise I'll answer."

"You happy with that smelter job?"

John snorted in disgust. "Hate it, Jim. Plan to give it a few more months, then quit. Why do you ask?"

"Just thinking. You used to be a lawman, didn't you?"

"Sort of. For a while."

Burns poured himself a drink, lifted it toward John. "Hang around El Paso a spell, John. I've been doing some thinking. I believe this town could use you. It'll take a while to set it up."

John raised his own glass. "Jim, I'm tired of moving around. El Paso's home now."

John Selman sat across from Jim Burns in the small office in back of the Red Light, and tried not to let his disappointment show.

"Sorry, John," Burns said. "I thought we had a lock on it. It was a close vote, but the city council decided to go with someone else for marshal."

Burns took two glasses and a bottle of rye whiskey from a

cabinet behind his desk. He poured a double shot into each glass and handed one to John. "The word I got was that some of the city fathers didn't want somebody with a gunfighter's reputation for the top lawman in El Paso. It was a split vote, I hear."

John shrugged and lifted his glass. "Don't worry about it, Jim. No need to apologize. I know you did your best for me, and I appreciate that."

Burns thumped his glass onto the desktop in disgust. "Dammit, John, Jim Burns keeps his promises to his friends. I'll get you in eventually. If these damn fools on the council won't appoint you, we'll get the citizens of El Paso to do it for them. I can swing the votes."

John nodded and extended his hand. "That's good enough for me, Jim."

El Paso
September 1891

The knock on the door brought John Selman awake with a start. He scooped his Colt from the holster on his headboard.

"Who's there?" he called.

"Joaquin Estrada, John Selman. I need your help."

John lowered the pistol, swung the door open, and greeted the Mexican with a handshake. "Welcome, *amigo*. Come in. What brings you to El Paso?" John read the exhaustion on Joaquin's face and gestured toward a chair. The mantel clock bonged twice.

Joaquin sank into the chair and sighed heavily. "Three days ago, *bandidos Americanos* stole fifty of our horses. Cesar was holding the *remuda* and was killed."

John covered his anger by stirring the coals in the cookstove and reaching for the can of Arbuckle's coffee on a shelf above.

"The horse thieves came north, across the Rio Grande. I do not know Texas, John Selman. My employer has given me two hundred American dollars to employ a tracker. If you are not occupied at the moment?"

"We'll get them."

The two men sat in silence until the coffee boiled. John added a dash of cold water to the pot to settle the grounds, then poured two cups. "How many thieves, Joaquin?"

"The tracks say seven."

"Then we will need some men."

"I have five *vaqueros* with me, camped outside of El Paso."

"That should be enough." John sipped at the coffee. As usual, he had made it too strong. "John Junior will go with us. He's sixteen now, a grown man. And nearly as good with a gun as you and I, Joaquin. We will ride at first light."

John Selman and his party cut the tracks of the horse thieves at Hueco Tanks northeast of El Paso. The tanks, natural rock formations which held deep pools of scarce water, were the only reliable water source for miles, especially when large numbers of animals were involved.

"Looks like they're taking their time about it," John Junior said after the group had tracked the stolen herd for four more hours. "Probably feel safe enough now that they're in Texas."

"They won't feel so damn safe in a couple of days," John Selman said.

John Selman led his weary posse down the main street of El Paso. Four bodies were tied across saddles, three men roped together by the neck, hands bound to saddle horns. John Junior and Joaquin Estrada followed the prisoners, rifles at the ready. A crowd of curious onlookers gathered as the horsemen stopped at the El Paso jail.

John swung from the saddle as the jail door opened.

"Got some new residents for you, Irv." He jabbed a thumb toward the bound men. "Charge is horse theft. Mister Estrada here will sign the formal complaint."

An hour later John stood outside the courthouse, John Junior at his side. The two men were at the center of a sizeable group of El Paso citizens.

"How many of them were there, John?" someone in the crowd asked.

"Seven. We got them all."

"Why didn't you just hang those three you brought in?"

John shrugged. "Would have in the old days. But John Junior

here reminded me it's the nineties now. We have courts to handle such things."

"How about the horses?"

"Recovered all fifty. Estrada's *vaqueros* are herding them back to Mexico." John's gaze was drawn to one man at the edge of the gathering. He was a big man, wearing a gray wool suit and a derby hat. A frown creased his face. He looked vaguely familiar, John thought, but he couldn't put a name or a place to him.

Joaquin Estrada emerged from the courthouse, elbowed his way to John, and extended a hand. *"Gracias, amigo."*

"De nada. I would be glad to buy you a drink, Joaquin. With your employer's money."

Estrada shook his head. "There is no time, John. I must catch up with my horse herd. Another time, perhaps. *Adiós."* Estrada swung aboard his rangy sorrel and kneed the horse toward the Rio Grande crossing.

John Selman turned to John Junior. "Join me in a drink, son? You've earned it."

John Junior shook his head. "No thanks, Dad. I'm tired and I'll be expected back at work tomorrow now that the fun's over. I'll take care of the horses and turn in early. Leave you some supper on the stove."

John watched his son stride away. The young man showed little evidence of the long hours in the saddle, or of strain from the running gunfight. *Strange that two brothers should be so different,* John thought. *John Junior's almost a mirror image of me, but Bud's got no real talent with guns or taste for the hunt. A lot of his mother in him, likes the quiet life and security of a steady job.*

Word of the chase and capture of the horse thieves spread quickly through the streets of El Paso. John had no shortage of drinking partners that night. He had planned to spend his money at the Red Light, but wound up instead at the Mint Saloon. It was closer to the courthouse.

The sun had dropped below the western mountains when John waved off another drink and took his last roll with the dice. He had thrown a seven, and his point was nine. Crapped out. Which was the way he felt. Exhaustion and a couple of drinks too many blurred his thinking. He knew it was time to go home.

He breathed deep, letting the wash of cool night air chase the cobwebs from his brain as he neared Second Street on his way home. He had just stepped past the darkened entrance of a livery stable when something exploded against the right side of his face. John staggered, felt himself falling, saw the glint of light on metal, caught a fuzzy glimpse of a derby hat. Then the world went black as a searing pain slammed through the back of his mouth.

John struggled to consciousness and was greeted by a stab of agony the likes of which he had never before felt. He tried to speak. The words came out as a soft gurgle. He felt a hand on his shoulder.

"Easy, Dad." Bud Selman's voice was soft in John's ear. "You've had a rough time of it."

"Whaa—" John raised a hand to his face. It was heavily bandaged. Bud pulled his hand away.

"Don't try to talk. Someone jumped you on the way home last night. Doctor says it looks like you got clubbed in the face—your nose is broken, maybe the cheekbone, too. And you had a knife stuck halfway through your throat. It went in between your teeth and into the back of your mouth. You lost a lot of blood. Doc thought at first your throat had been cut."

"Man—gray suit—derby." The pain reached a peak even John Selman's will could not climb. He let himself slide back into the comfort of the red mist and the darkness which followed.

El Paso
November 1892

John Selman stood at Jim Burns's side at the front door of the Red Light Saloon and greeted each Mexican who had come to the big fiesta. The party was being hosted by Burns in John's honor as a candidate for constable in El Paso's general election the next day.

John could smile and laugh without pain now. His recovery had been slow agony at first, mere torture later. Finally he had regained his health enough to go back to work, this time as a trail drive and range boss for the Moore and Irvin brand and later for A. B. Fall, the New Mexico lawyer and rancher.

Jim Burns's message had caught up with him in the Tularosa Basin and summoned him back to El Paso with barely enough time to start campaigning for the office.

"We got a late start, John," Burns said, "but, by God, we'll show these goat-assed Republicans how to win an election."

The shrewd saloon owner knew John already had a goodly number of votes in the bank. The old gunfighter had plenty of supporters among El Paso's Anglo population. The key now was the Mexican vote, and among the Mexicans John Selman was a proven friend. Burns knew of the many favors he had done for the Mexicans over the years. Now it was time to call in a few.

John Junior stood alongside his father, chatting fluently in Spanish with a number of Mexicans, when Burns tapped the elder Selman on the shoulder.

"John, it's time we had a drink," Burns said. "There are some people at the bar I want you to meet." He reached behind the door and handed John Junior a new axe handle. "Stand guard here, Young John," Burns said. "Don't let anybody in who isn't of voting age. Once in, if any of them try to leave, hit them over the head with this until you make damn good Democrats out of them."

The fiesta lasted until the small hours of the morning. As the guests began to depart, John Junior stopped each man and showed him a sample ballot. The Democratic candidate column was marked with a rooster atop the list. *"El gallo, el gallo,"* John Junior said emphatically, pointing to the rooster.

Not a single Mexican male left the Red Light without repeating *el gallo* several times.

As he closed the door behind the final guest, Jim Burns chuckled. "They'll remember the rooster. Tomorrow morning, we send hacks to pick them up and take them to the polling places. They are our down-card ace in this political poker game." The saloon owner poured hefty drinks for himself, John, and John Junior, then raised his glass in a salute. "I promised you, John Selman, that I'd get you elected as a lawman in El Paso. Here's to our next constable."

When the votes were counted the next day, John Selman had won the constable race by 88 out of 1,486 ballots cast.

The *El Paso Times* headlined its story:

DEMOCRATIC PARTY
MAKES CLEAN SWEEP
The Country Is Safe

On November 15, with a crowd of friends and his two sons standing by, John Selman posted a $1,500 bond, took the oath of office, and pinned the constable's badge to his vest.

El Paso
May 1893

"Uncle John! Uncle John!"

John Selman turned in the saddle and grinned. A trio of youngsters ran toward him, barefoot and ragged in the sandy street of the poorest section of El Paso.

"Oh, no! *Bandidos!* I must ride for the hills," John cried out in mock fear. He pulled the dun gelding to a stop and waited for the three boys to catch up.

Paco was the first to arrive, the swiftest runner of the three. Paco had been the first to call the constable "Uncle John." The tag had stuck until most of El Paso now referred to John by that title.

Paco laughed at the standing joke between the two. John held his hands in the air in pretend surrender. "Be merciful, *bandidos*. All I have in the world is some hard candy in my shirt pocket. Spare my life and it is yours."

"Done," Paco said, his nine-year-old face now set and stern.

John stepped down from the saddle, squatted in the street, and nodded to the other two boys. "I know these *bandidos* who ride with you, Paco. Maximillian Onate and Joe Bob Rice. Bad *hombres*." John waited patiently until Paco had lifted three pieces of candy from his shirt pocket, then stood and shrugged, a woeful expression on his face. "Robbed again. The streets of El Paso are no longer safe."

"Can I ride your horse, Uncle John?" Joe Bob asked.

"Sure." John boosted the boy into the saddle. His short legs stuck almost straight out from the saddle seat.

"Tell us a story, Uncle John," Maximillian begged.

John pursed his lips as though in deep thought. "I will tell you a secret, but you must promise not to tell anyone else."

Three young heads nodded in excited agreement.

"It is not well known, this story. You have heard of the Western Trail, where cowboys once moved Longhorns to market? Well, I was there, in a place called Fort Griffin, when that trail was broken." John glanced around as if to make sure no one else was listening. "Here is that secret: cattlemen did not break that trail. It was the grandfather of young Maximillian here. He was a great hunter and all the animals feared him."

John paused until he was sure the three youngsters were completely engrossed in the yarn. "*Señor* Onate one day took his fine gun and went to hunt. He frightened a fierce animal. Soon, a great stampede of ferocious animals—many of them from the plains near El Paso—thundered away in terror to the north. It was that stampede of fierce armadillos that broke the Western Trail for the cowboys."

Uncle John Selman laughed with the others at the sheer absurdity of the yarn.

The youngsters he met in his rounds were the high point of his day. John had come to realize at his advanced age that he really *liked* kids. They were fun and honest. Painfully honest, sometimes.

He chatted with the boys for a quarter hour, then plucked Joe Bob from the saddle. "It is good to see you, my friends," he said, "but I have to go to work now."

John mounted, waved goodbye, and reined the dun toward downtown El Paso. There he would check the latest Wanted posters and assignments on the chalkboard in the police chief's office before beginning his rounds.

John Selman liked his job and knew he was good at it. The constable's post paid no set wage, but it provided a comfortable living from fees and shares of fines, usually for petty offenses.

Disturbing the peace, drunkenness, minor theft, and swearing at an officer of the law led John's list of arrests.

He and his sons had moved from the house on Santa Fe to better quarters on Sonora Street. John had also pooled his resources with Jim Burns, and the two shared interest in two hundred forty acres along the Rio Grande.

Best of all was that John Junior had been named to the El Paso police force and given the same beat as his father. The two frequently made rounds together. Bud stayed out of the limelight, content to work his way up in El Paso's growing business community.

John was amused by the fact that one of El Paso's biggest income producers was the Tenderloin District. Prostitution and gambling accounted for a hefty percentage of the El Paso economy. But some of the more upstanding citizens took offense at the enterprises. Under growing pressure to clean up the offending activities, the city fathers had reached a compromise.

Gambling was now permitted in any saloon or gaming house, but the ladies of the evening were limited to a specific area of town, where they had to pay fees to ply their trade. That section of town had been dubbed the Tenderloin before the ink dried on the new law.

It was a good arrangement for all concerned, John had to admit. It preserved a valuable economic asset to the community, while concentrating most such activity out of sight of the more conservative residential and trade areas.

The Tenderloin was also a rich source of income for a dedicated constable. John's daily earnings from fees and fines almost doubled when he patrolled the rowdy district.

As he rode, his gaze swept the streets of El Paso. Every man in a gray suit and derby hat came under careful scrutiny. During John's long convalescence after the knife attack, John Junior and Jim Burns had been able to turn up enough information to link the man and another accomplice to the gang that had stolen Joaquin Estrada's horses.

The man in the derby had not been seen since the night of the knife attack. That was unfinished business, and unfinished business was a sore that festered on John Selman. It was one of the things that kept him from being a contented man. That and the nights when he reached for Niconora and she wasn't there.

El Paso
April 1894

Constable John Selman leaned against the outside wall of a general store, keeping a watchful eye on busy Utah Street. El Paso had been well behaved today, almost as mild as the gentle spring evening.

John knew the calm wouldn't last.

Bass Outlaw was in town, and he had been drinking. It was a bad combination.

John had never been completely able to read Bass Outlaw. It was as if the little deputy marshal were two people. When he was sober, Bass Outlaw was one of the most likeable people John had ever known, quick of wit, gentle in nature, and a competent lawman. But whiskey turned Bass Outlaw inside out.

A few rounds of the bottle transformed the ex-ranger with the handlebar mustache into a hornet's nest waiting to be jostled. Bass Outlaw stood barely five-two in his handmade boots, and didn't weigh over a hundred-thirty. He was the deadliest small package John Selman had ever known. There was no way to predict what Bass would do when the whiskey got to him. His temper could turn nasty in a heartbeat and he was slick with a pistol, drunk or sober. Several men had found that out the hard way.

When Bass was in town, it was routine practice for the El Paso police department to assign someone to keep an eye on the little gunman. John Selman had drawn the Bass patrol today.

"Evenin', Uncle John."

John turned to the man who had just stepped from the general store and nodded a greeting. "Hello, Frank."

"Looks quiet tonight," Frank Collinson said. "You know Bass Outlaw's in town?"

"I know." John knew Collinson counted Outlaw among his friends. Outlaw had a lot of them, both in El Paso and in Alpine,

where he had landed a U.S. deputy marshal's badge after being
kicked out of the Texas Rangers for drinking on duty.

"Saw him earlier in the day," Collinson said. "He was hittin'
the bottle pretty hard. Went over to Tillie Howard's sportin'
house a while back to see Mary." Collinson chuckled. "That Mary
must be something if she can pull the kinks out of Bass."

John shoved himself away from the store wall. Bass Outlaw
wandered into view, his steps unsteady. Barnum's Show Saloon
was just around the corner. John knew at a glance that Bass had
stopped there to reload on Barnum's whiskey.

Bass spotted the two men and made his way toward them.
People in his path hurried to clear the way. It wasn't a bad idea.

Bass Outlaw stopped before John and Collinson. "Uncle John,
Frank," he said by way of greeting.

"Hello, Bass." John studied the gunman's eyes. They were
glazed and unfocused. "Heard you were in town as a witness in a
trial."

Outlaw grunted in disgust. "Trial, hell. They might as well go
ahead and hang the bastard. Save the state some money. C'mon,
fellows. Buy you a drink."

"Bass," Collinson said, "don't you think you've had enough?"

Outlaw spun toward Collinson. "*I'll* by God say when I've had
enough, Frank." There was an edge to Bass's voice and a snap to
his eyes that John Selman didn't like.

"Easy, Bass." John kept his voice steady and calm. "Nobody's
trying to tell you what to do. But Frank may be right. I think it
would be a good idea if you went to your hotel room and slept it
off."

Bass wavered slightly on his feet. "Sleep it off, hell." The surly
set of his face shifted abruptly into a grin. "My hair's just gettin'
curly again." He closed one eye in a lecherous wink. "I'm gettin'
an itch to take Mary on another little hayride."

John forced an answering smile. The best way to handle Bass
right now would be to humor him, let Mary settle him down
again. "Might not be such a bad idea, Bass. We'll stroll along with
you."

Bass cuffed Selman lightly on the shoulder. "Gonna cut yourself a filly out of her herd, Uncle John?"

John shook his head. "No. I'm getting too old for that sort of thing. Frank and I'll just have a drink, then go on about our business."

A half hour later, John and Frank Collinson were seated in Tillie Howard's parlor, glasses on a low table before them. Bass Outlaw had tossed back a single shot, then wandered off to Tillie's washroom to "fresh up" before knocking on Mary's door.

Tillie Howard's house brand was good whiskey, not the rotgut served in most places in the Tenderloin District, John thought idly.

The blast of a pistol brought Collinson half out of his chair. "Easy, Frank," John said. "Chances are Bass dropped his gun." He pushed his drink aside and rose. "I'll go check on him."

John was barely on his feet when a piercing whistle sounded from the back of the house. Tillie had bolted out the back door at the sound of the shot and was sounding the alarm that would bring lawmen to the sporting house.

"Damn, Tillie," John muttered as he sprinted toward the sound, "you're just going to cause more trouble."

John reached the back porch in time to see Tillie Howard duck away from Bass Outlaw, who was trying to grab the whistle. At the same time, Texas Ranger Joe McKidrict stepped into the backyard.

"It was nothing, Joe," John called to the ranger, "just an accident. Bass will be all right."

McKidrict, his pistol still holstered, stepped to Bass Outlaw's side. "Bass, why'd you shoot?"

Bass Outlaw's face flushed in rage. "You want some too, McKidrict?" He shoved the pistol muzzle against the ranger's head and pulled the trigger. McKidrict dropped. Outlaw fired a second shot into the ranger's back.

John hurdled the porch rail, drawing his own gun, and landed on his feet barely arm's length from the little outlaw. He saw Outlaw's gun barrel whip toward his face and knew his own draw was too late—

White light flashed across John's vision as Outlaw's pistol roared in John's face. The slug ripped past his ear. The muzzle flash all but blinded John; he fired by instinct at the hazy figure before him, and thought he saw Bass Outlaw stagger. John wiped a hand across his eyes in a desperate attempt to clear his vision.

LAST GUN **147**

He felt the slam of a bullet into his right leg above the knee, and another rip through his thigh. He went to his knees, still clawing at his eyes.

John saw only a blur as the gunman staggered backward, tumbled over Tillie Howard's back fence, then faded from sight. He felt a pair of strong hands under his armpits. "I can't see! Dammit, I can't see! Where's Bass?"

"Steady, Uncle John. You hit him. He isn't going far. We'll get you to the doctor." Frank Collinson lifted John Selman as easily as he would heft a rag doll.

It seemed to John Selman that the echoes of the gunshots kept rolling up and down Utah Street, growing louder, as Collinson lowered him into what seemed to be the back of a wagon. Then another blast of pain seared his face and leg, and carried him into darkness.

John Selman regained consciousness in time to see a faint blur of light before the doctor laid pads on his eyes and bound them into place.

"How bad is it?" John had trouble recognizing his own voice. "Am I blind?"

"No," the doctor said, his tone calm. "In time you'll regain most of the sight in both eyes. You caught a bad powder burn across them, but I didn't find any really severe damage. You'll probably experience a significant loss of night vision, though, Constable Selman."

John tried to relax, wondering why he felt so little pain, then decided the physician must have spooned some laudanum into him. "The leg?"

"That gave me the most trouble," the doctor said. "Bullet nicked an artery. We got that patched before you could bleed to death. We'll be measuring you for a cane, but that's better than measuring you for a casket."

"What about McKidrict and Bass?"

"McKidrict's dead, John." Collinson's voice came from nearby. "Bass won't make it through the night. You nailed him in the chest. Slug tore a lung all to hell. They put him in a whore's bed in the back of the Barnum saloon. Doctor says he hasn't got a chance."

John winced at a lance of pain in his leg. The laudanum was beginning to wear off. "Damn shame about McKidrict," he said. "Bass too, for that matter. He wasn't so bad when he left the bottle alone."

El Paso
October 1894

John Selman sat at the defendant's table in Judge C. N. Buckler's 94th District Court, trying to ignore the ache in his wounded leg. His cane, which he now knew would be part of him for the rest of his life, leaned against his chair. His vision had returned, though at times the images were fuzzy, and at night he could hardly see at all. It was, he decided, about as good a trade as a man could make given the circumstances.

He was not overly concerned about the outcome of his trial on murder charges in Bass Outlaw's death. The little gunman had all but put the pistol to his own chest. Still, a man could never be sure how a jury trial would turn out. Especially when a couple of people who wanted to see John Selman dead sat in the jury box.

Judge Buckler was nearing the end of his charge to the jury. *At least,* John thought, *we'll know soon. In the old days it wouldn't even have gone this far. Sometimes this law and order business gets carried to damn silly extremes.*

He listened with care to the judge's instructions to the jury. Buckler was a fair man, and he understood the old ways. The letter of the law didn't always win out over justice in Buckler's court. And even if things didn't go right here, John could always appeal.

"Gentlemen of the jury," Judge Buckler said in conclusion, "there being no evidence before you that the defendant John Selman is guilty of the crime of which he is charged in the indictment in this case, you are hereby instructed to find the defendant not guilty."

John slumped with relief in his chair as the courtroom erupted —cheers from his friends, catcalls and jeers from the friends of Bass Outlaw, and a few derisive comments from people who didn't know Outlaw from Adam's off ox, but just didn't like John Selman. Some people could build a big hate out of a little fine.

John waited until the commotion quieted and the bailiffs cleared the courtroom, then reached for his cane, nodded an unspoken thanks to the judge, and limped outside. Better than two dozen well-wishers waited on the courthouse sidewalk to shake the hand of the man who killed Bass Outlaw.

John shook their hands even though he would have preferred to go straight home. Bass had asked for it, maybe even needed killing. But the shootout didn't sit well with John Selman. His name had been splashed all over newspapers from El Paso to Boston. It was the sort of fame he didn't want and didn't need. He didn't know how to answer their stupid questions:

"Were you scared, Uncle John?"

"Didn't have time to get scared." *No, son, I always crap in my pants on April fifth; family tradition.*

"What's it feel like to kill a man?"

"Not good." *A damn sight better than if he kills you.*

"What'll you do if Outlaw's friends come gunning for you?"

"Have to cross that bridge when I get to it." *Shoot the bastards in the back first if I know who they are.*

"Does it hurt to get shot?"

"It hurts like hell." *Go piss a grapefruit if you want to find out.*

"How many men have you killed, Uncle John?"

"Don't know. Man doesn't count things like that." *A bunch less than I'd like to, if you people don't shut up.*

The damn questions were always the same. At least now he didn't have to pay for his own drinks.

NINE

El Paso
February 1895

John Wesley Hardin, attorney for the prosecution, watched with interest as Uncle John Selman entered the courtroom where G. A. Frazer was standing trial for the attempted murder of Jim Miller.

The old man with the cane, Hardin mused, looked like anything but a gunfighter. In his boiled shirt, tailored suit, and polished shoes, walking with a pronounced limp as he escorted a prisoner to the stand, he resembled more a harmless old-timer rocking on a porch than a working lawman.

Wes Hardin knew Uncle John Selman was about as harmless as a stepped-on rattlesnake. A man didn't put twenty or more men underground and live to be Selman's age by being harmless. And he had killed Bass Outlaw. It took more than a greenhorn to pull off that trick.

Hardin had lost count of the men he himself had killed before fifteen years in prison mellowed his outlook. Some, he knew, reckoned the total at forty—including one he was rumored to have killed for snoring too loud. Hardin made no attempt to deny any of the deaths attributed to him. He enjoyed the notoriety. And when a gunman-turned-lawyer appeared before a jury box, such a reputation might help sway a few timid souls in their verdict.

Hardin nodded a greeting to Selman, who returned the gesture. The man seemed pleasant enough, Hardin thought. He suppressed a wry grin at the idea of two killers—representing maybe sixty or more dead men between them—standing side by side, one now a lawyer, the other a police officer, as the witness was sworn in. The irony of this meeting wasn't lost on Wes Hardin.

Hardin dismissed the thought from his mind as Selman moved away from the bench. He knew he needed all his concentration if he were to win his first case in El Paso, especially one in which the defendant had all the high cards.

Miller might be a distant cousin, but he had been dead wrong in this instance. "Killin' Jim" Miller had gone looking for Frazer with a shotgun. He found him, and Frazer had nearly killed Miller for his troubles. *Damn fool should have just shot Frazer in the back and been done with it,* Hardin thought. *But then I guess I'd be out a fee.*

Two days later the jury returned, announced they were unable to reach a verdict, and the judge declared a mistrial. Wes Hardin didn't kid himself that his eloquence in arguing the case had swung part of the jury. If anything had helped Miller's cause it was his lawyer's reputation with a Colt. Hardin paused on the sidewalk outside the courthouse, breathing in the sights and sounds of bustling El Paso.

"Well, Mister Hardin," one of the courtroom observers said at his side, "will you be going back to Junction now?"

Hardin grinned. "No. I like the looks of El Paso. Homicidal town. A criminal lawyer should be able to make a good living around here."

Within the week Wes Hardin had found a second-story office for rent less than a block from the Gem Saloon on South El Paso Street. The Gem provided a potentially rich source of clients, with its penchant for attracting hardcases. It also offered the highest-stakes games in the gambling rooms on the second floor. The best of two worlds, Hardin told himself as he shoved a law book onto a shelf behind a sturdy desk. The kind of place a man could spend the rest of his life in comfort.

El Paso
April 1895

Wes Hardin sat behind a desk cluttered with legal papers and
wondered what the hell was wrong with the citizens of El Paso.
*Lord knows there's enough law business in this town, but I haven't seen
much of it. Two months gone and barely enough business for beer money.*
The clutter on the desk was mostly for show.

His business cards were scattered all over town, announcing
the availability of his services, and nobody seemed interested. He
had spent twelve of his fifteen years in prison studying law, and
passed the bar exam easily, but now all he had to show for his
efforts was a snub-nosed Colt thirty-eight and an engraved watch
given to him by a grateful Jim Miller. And less than a hundred
dollars cash.

At least, he thought, the lack of business had given him time to
work on his memoirs. He glanced up at the knock on his door,
mildly surprised. It was a rare sound.

"Come in," he called. He flipped open a law book and scanned
a page, hoping to appear busy.

He pushed back his chair and stood as a woman stepped into
the room. Her face bordered on the plain, but the rest of her
more than made up the difference. The dark green dress would
have been somber on most women, but on her it merely empha-
sized the full breasts beneath, the narrow, nipped waist, and lush
swell of hips. Some men could judge the nature of a horse just by
looking at it; Wes Hardin had the same gift with women.

"Pardon me for staring, madam," he said, "but it is seldom
such a presence graces these spare offices." He pulled a chair
from against the wall and placed it alongside the desk. "Please
have a seat. John Wesley Hardin, attorney, at your service."

He held the chair as the woman sat, then returned to his own
seat. "How may I help you, madam?"

"I need a lawyer." Her voice was husky and rich. Below the
folds of the green dress, Hardin glimpsed a slender ankle swell
into a full and shapely lower calf of pale skin as she crossed her

legs. He felt the familiar stirrings. *This one is a hell of a woman,* he thought. *A bear-cat between the sheets if I've ever seen one.*

"My name is Helen Beulah Morose. Perhaps you've heard of my husband, Martin Morose?"

"I've heard the name, Missus Morose," Hardin said, "but I must admit I'm not all that familiar with your husband's case. He is a fugitive, isn't he?"

Helen Beulah Morose nodded. "He has been hounded into Mexico by men who hate him. I wish to secure your services to make sure he is treated fairly."

"It would be my pleasure to serve you, Missus Morose. Now, if you would please refresh my memory on your husband's case?"

Wes Hardin had heard talk in the saloon about Martin Morose's escapades with the law. According to the rumors, Morose was a small-time rustler who fancied himself a terror as an outlaw. He ran with a thief and gunman named Vic Queen. The two had worn out their welcome in New Mexico and earned a bounty on their heads in the process.

Hardin made a steeple of his fingers and peered over their tips at Helen Beulah Morose.

The blonde's story confirmed the rumors. Morose and Queen had barely made it across the Rio Grande ahead of the New Mexico authorities. Reward posters were up on Morose, at a thousand dollars, and Queen at five hundred. New Mexico lawmen had filed a complaint against the two with El Paso authorities, and had filed extradition papers in Mexico. It seemed only a matter of time until Mexican authorities arrested the two and booted them back across the river.

"Of course, I am prepared to pay your fees in cash," the woman said. "Martin left me a substantial sum. In addition, a rancher named McKenzie went to Juarez and gave Martin four thousand dollars. He is to use the money to become a citizen of Mexico, and thus beyond the reach of American authorities." Helen Beulah Morose shifted in her chair. "Mister McKenzie prefers that Martin not stand trial." Her lips lifted in a knowing smile. "I think what Martin might say could be embarrassing to Mister McKenzie."

"I understand, Missus Morose," Hardin said, his concentration now divided between the woman and the growing amount of money involved.

He turned away and stared out the window, rubbing his chin as if in deep contemplation. Then he turned back to Mrs. Morose and flashed his most engaging smile.

"I think I may be able to help you." He made sure his voice sounded confident. "The question of your husband's citizenship should give us some leverage if he is somehow returned to Texas. In the meantime, we can begin other efforts."

"I would be most grateful, Mister Hardin." She reached into her purse and produced a stack of bills. "This is an advance on your fees for services. I trust five hundred dollars is sufficient to begin?"

"Quite sufficient." Hardin tucked the money into a pocket, not bothering to count it. He forced a frown. "Missus Morose, there are some fine points of law we need to discuss further. Perhaps you would join me for dinner tonight?"

Helen Beulah Morose smiled and nodded. Wes Hardin read the interest and the open invitation in the blue eyes. "I would be honored, Mister Hardin."

"Please. Call me Wes. 'Mister' is such a formal title."

"Very well. *My* friends call me Beulah." She stood and straighted her dress. "I'm staying at the Bright Hotel off San Antonio Street."

Wes Hardin bowed as he opened the door. "I know where it is. About six o'clock, then, Beulah?"

"Yes. That would be fine."

Wes Hardin closed the door gently after watching Helen Beulah Morose stride down the stairs, hips swaying. *All that money and a woman like that too,* he thought. *Wes, you've done all right by yourself today.*

Helen Beulah Morose stood for a moment in the sun-washed street. The itch of excitement that had begun when she stepped into Wes Hardin's office had grown and spread during the interview.

She had not expected the physical attraction she felt toward the gunfighter-turned-lawyer. For most of her adult life, Beulah Morose had made a fair living selling her body. Only on rare occasions had she enjoyed the act; it was simply what she did. Wes

Hardin, though, would be one of those exceptions. She could feel it. Hardin was a handsome man still in his prime, with a deep and muscular chest, strong arms, and eyes that said he knew how to please a woman.

Martin Morose fancied himself a ladies' man. Wes Hardin didn't have to fancy a thing, Beulah thought. She knew men. A woman didn't practice her line of work and not know them.

She strode down the street, her hip-sway less pronounced now that she was out of the line of sight of Hardin's office window. She was humming softly. She had found more than she had expected.

Beulah felt no sense of loyalty to the small-time outlaw she had married after a nightlong battle with the bottle. She did, however, have more than a casual sense of loyalty to his money—more than five thousand dollars. She was, Beulah told herself once more, entitled to at least half. She wanted all of it. It was more money than she had seen at one time in her entire life. Now she had the tool to get it. Wes Hardin. If the lawyer in him couldn't find a way, then the gunman in him could. Beulah Morose knew she was a woman who could handle both the lawyer and the gunman. The unexpected bonus was that she could enjoy herself at the same time.

El Paso Police Chief Jeff Milton hitched his chair closer to the table in the Wigwam Saloon and poured a fresh drink for the man seated across from him. United States Deputy Marshal George Scarborough nodded his thanks and sipped at the whiskey.

"George, it's time we brought this thing with Martin Morose to a head," Milton said, "and I think I've got an idea how we can do it."

Scarborough raised an eyebrow. "I'm listening, Jeff."

Milton toyed with his glass for a moment. "We need three more men. That ranger brother-in-law of yours, Frank McMahon, John Selman, and Wes Hardin." He raised a hand to ward off Scarborough's objection. "I know you and Wes don't get along, that he's bad-mouthed you a couple of times. Hear me out, George. Now, Uncle John hasn't much use for me either—and maybe not for Wes Hardin. It's hard to tell with those two, but they seem to be tolerating each other for now. You've been friends with Uncle John Selman for a long time, and whatever else he is, Selman stands with his friends." Milton refilled the glasses. "If you can convince Uncle John to go along with us, I can handle Wes."

Scarborough pursed his lips. "I don't know, Jeff. That's quite a mix to stir up into a posse. If anything goes wrong, there could be a lot of blood spilled."

Milton smiled. "Money smooths a lot of rough roads, Jeff. The reward is still out on Morose. And in addition to the thousand on his head, I've got good sources that say Morose is carrying over four thousand dollars in cash."

The police chief let Scarborough chew on that figure for a moment. "Think about this, George. Morose hates Hardin's guts. Hell, I would too, if he was sleeping with my wife and neither of them trying to hide it. That gives us an edge, another reason for Morose to come across the bridge. The man's not too bright. He just might be dumb enough to think we can set it up so he can take Hardin."

"And then we arrest him?"

"No, George. Then we kill him. Take the money and split it up. Nobody's going to raise a stink if Morose gets shot to pieces. After all, we're duly-appointed officers of the law—you, me, Uncle John, McMahon—and Morose *is* a fugitive from justice."

Scarborough raised his glass. "Looks like you've got all the angles figured, Jeff. I can get Uncle John to go along with the idea."

Jeff Milton lifted his own glass, touched the rim to Scarborough's. "Here's to Martin Morose, then. And to the prosperity he'll bring us all."

John Selman tried to focus his vision on the bottle on George Scarborough's table. The blurred words on the label kept running together. One thing to be said for George, John thought, the man didn't shave nickels when it came to buying good whiskey. This stuff went down easy and kicked like an Arkansas mule.

"I don't know, George." John tried to frame his words with care. His tongue didn't seem to want to cooperate tonight. "I got no objection to killing a man needs killing. But this is more like an execution. I'm not sure I like the setup."

George Scarborough toyed with his cigar. "Some things about

it I don't like myself, Uncle John. But it's a good plan. Nobody's going to raise a stink about Martin Morose. Why should all that money be wasted on a two-bit outlaw?" Scarborough took a drag from his cigar and let the smoke trickle out. "John, you and I have to start making plans for what we do when we're too old to chase drunks and outlaws. Now, I don't know about you, but I'm having trouble getting a nest egg together on a lawman's pay."

John glared at the bottle for a moment. "Something to think about, George. I been enough burden to my boys already. Don't want to drag them down in my old age, too." He twirled his glass between his fingers. "Man ought to have something to show for a lifetime, true enough." John sighed. "You're right, George. Won't be long until I have to face up to retirement, some drunk don't shoot me first."

"There's a lot of money involved in this," Scarborough said. "The reward's just penny ante. It's his roll that will set us all up."

John rubbed a hand across the back of his neck. He could feel the sweat on his brow, and his cheeks had gone numb from the whiskey.

"John, we need you." Scarborough leaned forward, his elbows on the table. "I'll try to get Morose to come across the river alone, but what if he brings some friends? We'd need every gun we could get." The marshal decided it was time to play his ace. "John, if any shooting starts I want a friend at my side, a man I can trust. A man who can handle a gun. I want you there."

John sighed. "Answer one more question, George, and I'll tell you whether I'm playing or not." He lifted his gaze to the marshal's face. "What the hell do we need Wes Hardin for?"

Scarborough chuckled. "Easy enough to answer, John. Beulah Morose is the key to the whole shooting match. Wes Hardin has the whore." He dragged on the cigar and sent a smoke ring drifting lazily toward the ceiling. "And if something goes wrong —say an official investigation—do you think a jury is going to believe Wes Hardin or us? Will they believe a man who's killed forty men, or will they believe four duly-sworn officers of the law?"

John Selman ran the proposition through his head once more.

Damn, that's a lot of money—something to leave my boys when I'm gone.
He made up his mind.

"All right, George. Count me in."

Railway Bridge, El Paso
June 1895

George Scarborough stood at the south end of the Mexican Central Railway bridge that linked El Paso and Juarez. In the faint light of a sliver of jaded moon, he studied the broad face of the bulky six-foot outlaw Martin Morose.

It had taken some heavy talking before he was able to convince Morose that a late-night visit to El Paso would be in Morose's best interest. And still more talking to convince the fugitive to bring a hefty amount of cash to use as a bargaining chip with Helen Beulah Morose. The final nail in the coffin proved Jeff Milton to be right; Morose was still in a jealous rage directed at Wes Hardin. A promised shot at the lawyer-gunman had brought Morose to the spot near the Texas boundary.

"Are you ready, Martin? Are you armed?"

"Ready, George. Pistol in my belt. To kill the bastard Hardin after I see my Beulah." The accent of his native Poland still lay heavy in Martin Morose's speech. "Are you sure nobody else knows about this?"

"You have my word on it, Martin. I'll lead the way."

Scarborough turned and stepped onto the bridge. He could hear the heavy tread of Morose's farmer-style shoes on the planks behind him. The trip across the bridge seemed interminable to George Scarborough. Sweat stitched his upper lip despite the slight chill of the night. If anything spooked Morose, the fugitive wouldn't hesitate to put a slug in the marshal's back. Scarborough could only trust in the men who waited on the other side to shoot straight and make it count.

The ambush had been planned with care. Uncle John Selman stood as lookout on the road to the bridge, ready to use his constable's authority to turn back any late travelers. Milton, Mc-

Mahon, and Wes Hardin waited in the tall reeds and brush on the Texas side of the bridge.

Scarborough increased his pace, opening the space between himself and Morose to four strides as he stepped off the end of the bridge onto Texas soil.

Morose was three steps into Texas when gunshots blasted from the roadside. Scarborough crouched and whirled as he drew his handgun.

Martin Morose staggered, riddled by rifle and pistol bullets and buckshot, then fell into the middle of the road. He struggled to one knee, managed to pull his handgun, then went down again under a second volley. Scarborough fired once into the twitching figure. Wes Hardin sprinted from the brush to Morose's side, put a boot in the big man's back, and fired almost point-blank into Morose's neck. He slid a hand beneath the riddled body. The hand emerged holding a thick sheaf of bills.

"We'll split later," Hardin half whispered as Scarborough stepped to his side. Hardin picked up Morose's pistol, fired a shot into the air, re-cocked the weapon, and placed it by the dead man's hand. He then walked rapidly back toward town. Milton and McMahon headed for the Tenderlon District, reloading weapons as they moved.

George Scarborough had no time to argue with Hardin. And if he'd had the time, he didn't have the inclination. Facing Wes Hardin when the lawyer had a fistful of pistol wasn't the smartest thing a man could do. Besides, Scarborough knew his work was not yet done. He heard the calls from the outskirts of El Paso, saw torches heading toward the bridge. Selman, according to plan, would join the crowd; the two officers would "investigate" the shooting.

Scarborough toed the blood-soaked body in the road. The reward and his share of the money taken from Martin Morose's body would be substantial. All in all, he figured, not a bad night's work.

John Wesley Hardin yawned, stretched, and let his hand fall on Beulah's bare breast. She lay on the bed at his side.

"Well, Widow Morose," he said with a grin, "how does it feel to be a free woman again?"

Beulah snuggled closer against him. "Free and rich. Not a bad combination, Wes." She was silent for a moment as her fingers traced random outlines on Hardin's belly. "Wes, that money you took off Martin. It's mine—ours—you know. There's no need to share with any of the others."

Wes Hardin chuckled. "Never intended to share, Beulah. And I don't think there's a man among them with guts enough to try to take it from ole John Wesley Hardin. Reputation's a good thing sometimes." He felt a stirring at his crotch, under Beulah's fingers. "Guess we better get dressed to attend poor old Martin's funeral. After all, he was my client and your husband."

Beulah Morose let her lips brush Wes Hardin's neck. "There's plenty of time, Wes."

The city of El Paso paid scant attention to Martin Morose's funeral. The undertaker had to go into the streets and hire pallbearers. Only two mourners—Beulah Morose and her lover—were at Concordia Cemetery when the outlaw was laid to rest.

A week after the funeral, John Selman leaned against the bar in George Look's saloon and glared through the open door as Wes Hardin and Beulah Morose rode past in Beulah's coach.

"Appears Wes has turned pretty prosperous for a lawyer without any clients," Look said as he poured a fresh drink for John. It was Selman's fourth of the day, and noon was still an hour away.

"Hell yes, he's prosperous." The bitterness in John's voice caught Look by surprise. "He's got a hefty roll in his pocket. It was Martin Morose's roll."

George Look was about to ask John how he knew that, but thought better of it when he studied the constable's weathered face. The expression there reminded George of a coiled rattler looking for something to strike.

John Selman tossed off the last of his drink. *Damn Wes Hardin's soul,* he grumbled to himself. *He hasn't shared a dime of Morose's money. If he doesn't pony up pretty soon, I'm going to take it out of his hide.* He waved off George Look's gesture with a bottle. Whiskey was a fickle bitch, John mused. When things were going well, it was a silky lady to smooth the rough edges and relax a man; when things were going bad, it was a shrew who nagged and whined and dragged a man down until his mean side boiled over.

He pushed himself away from the bar. The whiskey was shrewish as hell today, he thought as he stepped into the haze of coal smoke and dust that sometimes smothered the city on hot, windless days.

George Look watched Uncle John limp through the saloon door, and shook his head. The constable was punishing the bottle more than usual these days. So far the whiskey hadn't clouded Selman's judgment as a lawman. But Look had seen enough heavy drinkers to know that someday something would snap. One thing he knew for sure. He'd hate to be in Uncle John Selman's way when it happened.

El Paso
July 4, 1895

El Paso seldom needed a reason to celebrate, but on Independence Day everybody turned the wolf loose.

It was still early afternoon and John Selman had already helped fill the El Paso lockup. Those arrested were merely the worst offenders. Minor infractions that would normally land a man in jail were handled with a fine collected on the spot, or the offender was dismissed with a stern warning.

John didn't mind the extra work the holiday brought. His share of fines and fees today would be the equal of two or three weeks' normal duties.

He limped along the crowded sidewalk. His head pounded from the constant barrage of drunken whoops, gunshots fired into the air, saloon pianos, and the occasional curses from the street jammed with horses and all manner of carriages and buggies. Before the night was out, John knew, the saloon keepers would be deep in cash, the prostitutes would have some indelicate sore spots to go along with their bulging purses, and it was possible the undertaker's wagon would need some wheel grease.

Despite it all, John enjoyed the Fourth. It brought back memories of his own wilder days. The days when he could howl with the best of them, before age and a collection of bullet holes slowed him down.

John paused at the edge of Washington Park, his attention caught by a series of gunshots. The muzzle blasts were not the random shots of celebration. They were evenly spaced, four measured shots at a time.

Curious, John moved into the park and soon found himself at the edge of a crowd. He recognized many of the faces as regulars at the Wigwam Saloon. Smokey Willis, whom John had pointed out to the Boston reporter as Billy the Kid, stood at the edge of the mob.

"What's all the commotion, Smokey?"

"Wes Hardin's puttin' on a shootin' show," Smokey said. He reached into a pocket and handed John a playing card. It was the three of diamonds. Three bullet holes had all but obliterated the center diamond, and a forth hole was punched just above the other three. Wes Hardin's initials and the date were penciled on the bottom of the card. "Some shootin', eh, John?"

John did not reply. He had seen Wes Hardin's calling card once before, tacked to a post in a Griffin saloon. It hadn't impressed him much back then. He handed the card back and shoved his way toward the front of the crowd, Smokey tagging close behind. John's jaw muscles tensed as he spotted Hardin. The lawyer was laughing and joking, the center of attention, and obviously enjoying the role.

Hardin aimed his Smith & Wesson forty-four toward a card tacked into the trunk of a tree fifteen feet away, and fired four shots. The crowd roared its approval. All four holes were near the center marker of what had been the ace of clubs. Hardin waited until a bar patron retrieved the card, then signed it with a flourish and a grin.

"Hey, Wes," Smokey called from John's side, "that's some fair pistol work. But I got five dollars says this man here can beat it." He clapped a hand on John Selman's shoulder. John shook off Smokey's grip in irritation.

Hardin's eyes narrowed as he stared at John. The gunman had been into the bottle, as usual, John noted. He read the challenge in Hardin's eyes.

"How about it, Uncle John?" Hardin's question was clear in the hush that fell over the crowd.

John returned Hardin's stare. "Not today, Wes."

A murmur of disappointment swept through the gathering.

"Afraid you can't top it, Constable?" someone asked.

"Don't see the point in it," John replied, his voice calm and steady. "Cards don't shoot back."

"What do you mean by that, Selman?" Anger colored Hardin's face.

"Make it what you will, Wes." A heavy tension settled over the crowd at the possibility of two veteran gunfighters going at each other. "I said what I felt." John struggled to control the powerful urge to reach for his Colt. "I've got things to do, Wes." John deliberately turned his back on Hardin. "No law against a shooting exhibition, boys," he said. "Just make sure nobody gets hurt."

The disappointed crowd parted in respect as John limped back toward the main street. He found himself wondering almost idly how the smart money would have gone if he'd called Hardin. It had been a near thing, but it wasn't the right time or place. Hardin still owed him some money . . . and you can't collect from a dead man.

TEN

El Paso
August 1895

El Paso Police Officer John Selman Junior sauntered along the sidewalk of San Antonio Street, part of his regular beat when he worked the night shift. The early evening had been quiet—as quiet as the saloon strip of El Paso ever was—and with the approach of midnight the carousing was beginning to flatten out.

John Junior paused to check the door of a feed store, found it solidly locked, and leaned against the doorjamb for a moment. He couldn't shake a nagging worry about his father. John Selman had never been a stranger to whiskey, but he had been hitting the bottle with a vengeance the past few weeks. He had also been spending more time at the gaming tables. The latter was notable mainly because John Selman was losing more than he was winning. John Junior couldn't help believing that John's gambling losses were connected to his preoccupation with John Wesley Hardin.

The lawyer's presence seemed to irritate John a bit more each day, like a thorn slowly festering in a horse's side. Yet in public, John Selman and Wes Hardin had seemed at least tolerant of each other when they were together.

The whole situation left John Junior confused. His father and Wes Hardin were not quite like two dogs with raised hackles, but there seemed to be an undercurrent of tension when they met. John Junior had been unable to talk to his father about it; when the name Hardin came up in private conversations between father and son, John Selman merely grunted and changed the subject.

For the moment, at least, it didn't matter. Hardin was out of town on one of his trips to New Mexico. John Junior wondered why the little town of Phenix drew so many people from El Paso. It was said the town was wild, but so was El Paso. A man didn't have to travel outside the city limits to find all the mischief he wanted.

John Junior sighed, pushed himself away from the doorjamb, and resumed his prowl of San Antonio Street. Whatever was gnawing at John Selman was behind a wall his son couldn't breach.

He was near Charlie's Restaurant when a female figure staggered onto the sidewalk. Helen Beulah Morose had taken on a snootful of liquor in Wes Hardin's absence. John Junior wasn't surprised. Beulah could hammer a bottle as hard as any man. There had been rumors she had sought pleasures other than the bottle when Wes was out of town.

"Hey, John Junior!" Beulah had trouble forming the words as she stood in the middle of the boardwalk, swaying as if in a gusty wind. She carried a parasol under her right arm. Her skirts were disheveled, her blouse rumpled. A loose strand of hair dangled in front of her right ear.

John stopped an arm's length from the woman. The glow from a window showed the blue eyes slightly out of focus, the smile on her face crooked. John Junior touched fingertips to his hat brim in greeting. "Evening, Missus Morose. It appears the spirits have gotten into you. Would you like an escort home?"

Beulah Morose giggled. "Home, my ass. Night's young, boy." Her grin faded. She peered hard into young John's face. "Tell you what, John Junior. I can outdrink, outcuss, and outshoot you or your old man. And by God, I'm gonna prove it! Let's you and me have us a shootin' contest, police boy."

"Missus Morose, you probably could outshoot me. There's no need to prove anything. Besides, we don't want to wake up the good citizens of El Paso." He smiled. "Come along. I'll help you home." He reached for her elbow.

"Keep your hands off me, you dammed little whelp, or I'll use you for a target!"

John Junior could handle a drunken cowboy or soldier, but he wasn't sure what to do with a woman flying three sheets to the wind. He did know that a woman's finger could pull a trigger as easily as a man's. The glint of light on metal in the folds of the parasol caught his eye. He reached out and whisked the little Smith & Wesson top-break thirty-two from its hiding place.

"Damn you, John Junior! You give me that gun back!"

"No, ma'am. I can't let you run around armed in this condition. You can have your gun back when you sober up."

Beulah Morose spat in John Junior's face, then launched into a tirade of curses that made a drover's language sound like Sunday preaching. John Junior's face flushed in growing anger. "All right, Missus Morose. You've stepped across the line. Nobody talks to me like that. You're under arrest for disturbing the peace and carrying a concealed weapon." He hooked a palm beneath the woman's elbow and half led, half dragged her toward the jail.

After Helen Beulah Morose was charged, jailed, and had passed out in a small cell in the El Paso lockup, John Junior sat at his desk and began filling in an arrest report. He glanced up as the part-time jailor chuckled aloud.

"What's your problem, Clint?"

"Just thinkin'," the jailor said. "Wild night in El Paso. Arrestin' a whore for cussin' out a policeman." Clint clucked in admiration. "Damn, that gal can cuss."

John Junior had to smile despite his lingering anger. "You should have heard her a few minutes ago. I learned some new words. And the way she put them together was almost poetry. It would have been entertaining if it hadn't been directed at me."

John Junior finished the report, signed it with his customary flourish, and rose to resume his beat.

"Young John, I sure hope you didn't make a mistake." The humor was gone from the jailor's tone. He nodded toward the back cell where Helen Beulah Morose slept. "You know that's Wes Hardin's whore?"

John Junior nodded. "I know who she is."

"Wes may not take kindly to that."

"Well, Clint," John said, "as my father once told John Wesley Hardin, he can take it any damn way he wants."

John Junior's final duty on that night's shift came early the next morning when he escorted the hungover and now contrite blonde before the El Paso Recorder's Court, where minor offenders were brought to justice.

Helen Beulah Morose apologized profusely to the court, and paid her fifty-dollar fine. Before leaving the court she turned to the young officer.

"Please forgive me, Officer Selman. I made a complete fool of myself and caused you embarrassment. It was the whiskey talking. I promise you it will never happen again."

John Selman Jr. nodded his acceptance of the apology. "As far as I am concerned, Missus Morose, the matter is closed."

John Wesley Hardin rode back into El Paso a day later, picked up two bottles at the Acme Saloon, and disappeared into the rented room he shared with Beulah Morose at Annie Williams's rooming house.

The talk around town was that Wes Hardin and Beulah Morose were riding a rocky road in their relationship. The battles between the two had become part of local legend. No one knew the cause of the problems, and nobody cared enough to risk stepping into the domestic conflict.

John Selman Jr. wound up in it anyway.

Helen Beulah Morose went before a justice of the peace two days after Wes Hardin's return. Annie Williams confirmed Beulah's account of a violent quarrel. Beulah told the judge that Hardin had threatened to kill her and make it appear to be suicide, but had passed out on the bed before carrying out the threat.

The justice of the peace issued a warrant for Wes Hardin's arrest for disturbing the peace.

John Selman Jr. and two other El Paso police officers found Wes Hardin the next morning in the Acme Saloon. Young John expected trouble, but Hardin surrendered meekly.

"Son, I'm so damn sick this morning I couldn't fight a banty rooster." Hardin handed his pistol to John Junior. "God, I've never had such a hangover in all my born days," he muttered as he was led to jail. "Bad whiskey's a hell of a way to die—"

After recuperating in the El Paso jail, Wes Hardin posted a peace bond of one hundred dollars in the justice of the peace court and was released. Constable John Selman watched the proceedings, then escorted Wes Hardin to the courthouse door.

Uncle John Selman leaned on his cane across the desk from Police Chief Jeff Milton. "You sent for me, Jeff?"

"Sit down, John. Leg still bother you?"

"No more than usual. What's on your mind?"

Jeff Milton stared into the old gunfighter's eyes. "Thought you should know, Uncle John. Wes Hardin's been making threats against your boy. He's sore over John Junior arresting Beulah Morose."

Milton saw John Selman's eyes narrow. "What's Hardin said?"

"That John Junior's life isn't worth a Confederate dollar in El Paso. He said it more than once, Uncle John. I heard him myself, in the Wigwam. Bartender at the Acme told George Scarborough the same thing."

Selman pushed himself erect on his stiff right leg. "We'll see about that, Jeff. Thanks for telling me."

Jeff Milton watched John Selman limp toward the door, shoulders set in anger. "One more thing, John," Milton said. "I heard Hardin say that after he took care of John Junior he was coming after you. I think his exact words were, 'I'll make the old bastard shit like a wolf all around the block.'"

John Selman didn't look back. He stepped into the street. He made no effort to check the rage that boiled inside.

He found Wes Hardin outside the Acme Saloon, lounging against a porch post. It was one of the rare occasions when Hardin was alone.

John stopped an arm's length from Wes Hardin. "I hear you've made some talk about my boy and me." John kept his voice low and his hand close to his holstered Colt. Hardin wasn't wearing a gunbelt, but John had never known Wes Hardin to be without a pistol, which he usually carried in the waistband of his trousers.

"We can settle it now, Hardin," John said. "Just step out into the street."

Wes Hardin's calm, almost disinterested gaze locked into John's eyes. "I have no quarrel with you, Selman. I don't want to fight you. I'd rather fight your son."

"You want to get to him, you go through me." John let his

thumb slip over the hammer of the Colt. "It's your call, Hardin. Put up your chips or fold."

Anger flashed in Hardin's eyes, then faded. He half smiled. "Let it slide, Uncle John. If I did any talking against John Junior, it was just whiskey talk. Besides, I've got a crap game waiting on me. Won't be any easy money left if I fool around too long."

Hardin turned his back and strode into the saloon. John Selman fought down the urge to pull the Colt and pop a couple into Hardin's back. He spun on a heel and stomped away.

El Paso
August 1895

"Dammit, George," John Selman snapped, "Hardin's gone too far this time. He's threatened my son but he won't fight me. George, I didn't raise that boy, nurse him through the pox, and mend his britches just to see him shot down like a mad dog on the street."

John's hand fell by instinct onto the butt of the forty-five at his hip. "Maybe Hardin *has* killed forty men. I'll promise you this before God—there won't be a Selman as number forty-one in Hardin's tally book."

Deputy Marshal George Scarborough twirled an unlighted cigar in his fingers and studied the flushed face of the old gunfighter. John Selman was up to three bottles of whiskey a day now. It didn't help his surly mood. The man was a powder keg looking for a spark.

"John, we can't arrest a man for talk. You know that."

"Then what the hell are you going to do?"

"Nothing, John. There are no warrants against Wes Hardin."

"Warrants," John snorted. "Who the hell needs a warrant? George, you know damn well Hardin's been running his mouth off about the Morose killing. He's all but told half of El Paso he hired you to gun down that half-assed outlaw."

"And after he sobered up, he apologized for it, John. In public and in the newspapers," Scarborough said. "Now, think about it for a minute. If we did charge him with something and put him on the stand, he'd start naming names on the Morose affair. We can't afford that.''

John Selman glared at the marshal for a long moment. ''Besides threatening my son, Hardin's still got the Morose money. If he hasn't gambled or whored it all away by now. A man who'd go back on his word like that doesn't deserve to live. By God, George''—John all but spat the words—''you people may stand for it, but I won't. He has to come across or I'll kill him.''

George Scarborough watched the old man stride away. Uncle John wasn't the only man Wes Hardin owed from the Morose deal. But it wasn't the easiest debt in town to collect. George himself had braced Hardin over it twice; the second time he'd wound up looking down the barrel of that forty-four Smith & Wesson Hardin carried. George didn't care to go through that experience again. The money seemed a hell of a lot less important after that. George knew he couldn't take Hardin in a gunfight, but somebody had to put the lawyer down before Hardin's whiskey talk stuck all their heads in a noose.

John Selman just might be that man.

If Selman pulled it off, he could be dealt with later. If Hardin was the one still standing, things could happen to a man in jail. *It would be damned interesting,* Scarborough thought, *to see which of the old gunmen came out alive.*

El Paso
August 1895

Uncle John Selman slumped at his customary table in the Wigwam Saloon, knuckles white under the black rage that churned in his gut as he gripped the whiskey glass. The bottle before him was almost empty.

When the bottle was drained, he would kill Wes Hardin.

It was the one final way to make sure Hardin wouldn't carry out his threats against John Junior. *Dammit, I've lost near everybody I ever loved; Hardin's not going to take John Junior away from me,* Selman vowed.

And there was the Morose money. John still hadn't seen a dime of it. That money would let an old constable retire in comfort. It would let him spend more time with Niconora, to make sure her grave was tended, and to be no burden to his sons in his last years. If someone didn't do something soon, there wouldn't be any of the Morose money left.

What galled Uncle John Selman as much as anything was that he had been used in the Morose killing. Used like an old saddle and then tossed aside. *Hardin, you played me like a cheap fiddle. I've let you get away with it too damn long already. No man plays John Selman for the fool.*

John's hatred of Hardin had been building for weeks. In the last few days it had become almost unbearable. *The arrogant sonof-abitch thinks he can do whatever he damn well pleases and get by with it. Thinks there's nobody in the whole of Texas will call him out. Well, by God, there's one man who isn't afraid of John Wesley Hardin.*

John dribbled the last of the amber liquid into his glass and thumped the empty bottle on the table. He raised the glass, watched the liquid swirl for a few seconds. *Here's to you, Wes Hardin, and may your soul burn in hell.* He tossed the whiskey down in one gulp.

John Selman pushed himself away from the table.

Outside, he checked the loads in the cylinder of his Colt Peacemaker and strode toward the Acme Saloon. Hardin would be there, just as he had been earlier in the day. Swilling free drinks from the hangers-on who wanted to be in the company of a "real gunfighter." *Enjoy your last few minutes, Hardin. There's a real man after your butt now.*

John Junior stepped alongside his father as the old gunman neared the Acme. "What's up, Dad?" he asked.

John Selman didn't look at his son. "Just taking care of a little problem. Wait outside, son."

John Selman peered across the top of the swinging doors. Wes Hardin and a grocer were playing a dice game at the bar four strides away. Hardin tossed the dice. "You have four sixes to beat," he said.

Selman slipped the Colt from its holster, cocked the weapon, and stepped through the swinging doors.

"Hardin!" John raised the pistol as he called out.

Hardin glanced over his shoulder. His eyes flared in surprise. Then he turned, a hand thrust toward his belt.

John Selman fired. The slug tore into Hardin's head and slammed his body against the bar. The gunman toppled to the floor. For an instant a shocked silence gripped the Acme Saloon, then the grocer barked a curse and flung himself to the floor. Furniture clattered as other patrons dove for cover or stormed toward the door. John took two steps forward, thumbing the Colt. As he fired again, someone bolting for the exit jostled John's shoulder and the slug ripped into the floor. He recovered his balance and, standing almost directly over Hardin's body, fired two more shots. Then someone grabbed John's arm, and forced the pistol aside.

"Don't shoot him anymore," John Junior said. "He's dead."

John Selman Jr. took the pistol from his father's hand. The old man's expression was locked in a scowl, a distant look in the cold blue eyes.

The Acme filled as rapidly as it had emptied. Someone knelt by Wes Hardin's body, and after some difficulty pulled a Smith & Wesson forty-four pistol from the dead man's waistband. "Snagged in his shirt," the man said. "Had it half drawn."

John Junior took his father's elbow. "Dad, I've got to put you under arrest."

John Selman blinked twice, as if fighting his way back to reality, and let his son lead him from the saloon. He still had not spoken.

Wes Hardin's body lay on the floor for better than an hour to accommodate the curious as word spread of the gunman's death. The body was finally taken to the undertaker on West Overland Street, where the blood and gore were washed away and the remains of John Wesley Hardin were prepared for photographers.

John Selman's first shot had torn into Hardin's head at the corner of the left eye. The second had hit the upper right arm, the third the right side of the chest just above the nipple.

On August 20, the *El Paso Herald* reported that Hardin's "features were in good shape and he looked well."

Constable John Selman, free on bond pending his trial for the murder of Wes Hardin, stood on a street corner and watched as two carriages and two buggies followed the undertaker's wagon bearing Hardin's body toward Concordia Cemetery. John's hat remained on his head, his hands folded over his chest, as the brief procession passed.

"Uncle John," a reporter from the *Herald* said at John's side, "you never have told anyone the whole story, have you? Why you killed John Wesley Hardin?"

John glanced at the reporter. "I've told the story. Wes Hardin threatened my life and the life of my son. There were a couple of other men he planned to kill." John sighed. "There was something else. I had information that Wes Hardin and some of his friends were going to rob the State National Bank. I went to the Acme to tell Hardin I was on to his plan." The lie sat easily on John's tongue. It was the kind of story El Paso would believe, and would make the Hardin killing seem as much a police job as a personal score settled.

The reporter's eyebrows arched in surprise. "That's the first time I've heard that, Uncle John."

"There's a lot about Wes Hardin you don't know, son." John made no offer of explanation. The reporter chose not to press the point.

"I have to ask, Uncle John. Everyone says you shot Wes Hardin in the back of the head. That doesn't seem like you."

John whirled to face the reporter. "Dammit, I'm tired of hearing that crap," he snapped. "I looked Wes Hardin square in the eye and shot him while he was reaching for his gun. Anybody who says otherwise is a damn liar!"

The reporter raised a hand. "I'm not the one doing the talking, Uncle John. Don't be angry with me. I've got to go now. Supposed to be covering Wes Hardin's funeral for the paper." The young man nodded a farewell to John, then hurried away to catch up with the procession en route to the cemetery.

"The real reason, son," John muttered toward the retreating figure, "is that the sonofabitch deserved killing. Pure and simple deserved it. Dammit, in the old days I wouldn't have even needed a reason for shooting a Wes Hardin or anyone else of his kind."

John Selman hitched up his trousers and continued his tour of San Antonio Street. He was still a constable of El Paso, with a beat to walk. At least until the trial.

El Paso
February 1896

Albert B. Fall, attorney for the defense, and Deputy Marshal George Scarborough stood at John Selman's side as Judge C. N. Buckler declared a mistrial.

The jury in John's trial for the murder of John Wesley Hardin had debated the issue for two days before reporting to the judge they were hopelessly deadlocked.

"This case will be rescheduled for the next term of this court," Judge Buckler said. "In the meantime, bond in the amount of one thousand dollars will be continued."

Fall turned to John Selman. The old man's eyes showed neither disappointment nor relief. "Well, Mister Selman," Fall said, "I fully expected a not-guilty verdict. But we made some points. And in the next trial, I think we should put you on the witness stand. Letting you tell your side of the story directly to the jury should carry enough impact to sway any undecided votes to your cause."

The attorney glanced at Scarborough and wondered why the marshal's eyes narrowed in a quick flash of concern. *No matter,* the attorney thought. *He's probably just worried that something might happen to John before the next trial.* The old constable didn't seem to be in the best of health. It was as though the quick, incisive mind Fall had known for several years had slipped—or perhaps stalled in time, frozen in the gunfire at the Acme Saloon.

El Paso
March 1896

Marshal George Scarborough had made it a point to stay as close as possible to John Selman, and what he saw was not reassuring.

The old constable was seldom sober these days, and had changed in other ways. He seldom smiled or laughed now. He was usually curt, sometimes downright surly. Scarborough had seen John Selman's bleak, dark moods before, but they rarely had lasted more than a day or two. Now people had stopped calling him Uncle John. Even the youngsters seemed to be avoiding him.

Maybe, Scarborough thought, it was the pressure of being the man who killed John Wesley Hardin. It was a bigger story than the Bass Outlaw killing. For a man like Selman, sudden nationwide fame would be like having his feet held to a forge. For the first time in his life John Selman was staring face to face at a problem he simply couldn't handle.

Hardly a day went by without a rumor that a new gun was in town, a gun looking for a reputation as the man who killed the man who had shot Wes Hardin. Selman paid no attention to the rumors. His sons did. One or the other stayed at his side most of the time, especially at night when the constable was almost blind.

George Scarborough also kept a sharp watch for new faces in town, but for a different reason. He was hoping a fast gun *would* show up. It would solve a lot of potential problems.

The marshal knew that the Morose affair was eating away at John Selman, and that it went beyond the money he had never collected. John had never been comfortable with his role in the Morose killing. It was like a cancer gnawing at the old man's gut.

George Scarborough now realized that John Selman was close to breaking. That was something he couldn't let happen.

El Paso
April 5, 1896

Deputy Marshal George Scarborough paused on the stairway leading down from the gaming rooms in the Wigwam Saloon. John Selman stood at the foot of the stairs, leaning against the balustrade.

Scarborough could tell at a glance that the old gunfighter was even more drunk than usual. This time, at least, he had a legitimate reason to hit the bottle.

John Junior was in big trouble. The young man had fallen for a Mexican girl and the two had eloped three days ago, fleeing on bicycles across the border with the intent to be married. The girl was fifteen. Her father objected, and now John Junior occupied a cell in the Juarez jail, charged with abduction. It wasn't a charge considered lightly in Mexico. Especially when the wounded father was a wealthy and politically powerful man.

Scarborough knew John had returned earlier in the day from a visit to the Juarez lockup.

"George, I need to talk to you." John's words stumbled a bit upon themselves. His face was lined in a deep frown. Tufts of hair protruded from beneath his hat. The old man was beginning to take on the appearance of a haggard vagabond, instead of the meticulous dresser George Scarborough had known.

Scarborough draped an arm across John's shoulders. "Sure, John."

"It's about John Junior. It's going to take a lot of money to get him out, George." John's voice was low, the tone urgent. "The trial cost me nearly everything I had. I'm nearly broke now. You must know where the Morose money is. I need my share and I need it now. You know how much that boy means to me."

George Scarborough winced inwardly. The time he had dreaded—and feared—had come. Selman was desperate, and drunk to boot. It was a combination that could blow the lid off the Morose murder. There were a lot of people who couldn't afford that.

Scarborough forced a grin and glanced around. The Wigwam was almost deserted, as it should be at four in the morning on Easter Sunday.

Scarborough gave the wiry shoulders a protective squeeze. "I bet I can help you out, Uncle John. Tell you what—let's go out in the alley where none of these barflies can overhear us."

The marshal opened the back door and let John Selman lead the way into the alley. As the door closed behind them, Scarborough pulled his forty-five.

Scarborough's first shot plowed a bloody furrow across John Selman's neck. The old gunman staggered. "George, no! Don't kill me like that!" John cried out. A second slug tore into his side. His legs collapsed and he fell. Two more gunshots rattled through the alley.

El Paso
April 6, 1896

Bud Selman stood at his father's side in Sisters Hospital. The old man lay face-down on a surgical table, his features twisted in agony despite the opium daze. The pain killer was no match for the bullet lodged against John Selman's spine.

"Bud." John's voice was a faint whisper. "He—never gave me chance—to pull my gun."

Two surgeons appeared before Bud could reply. "We're ready to operate, Uncle John," one of the doctors said.

"Then—cut and—be done with it." John Selman's breath came in short, labored gasps. "I'd rather die than—be a cripple—rest of my life."

"You'll have to wait outside, Bud," the surgeon said with a curt nod toward the door.

An hour later, Bud rose from his seat on a bare bench in the waiting room as a surgeon, his smock steaked with blood, pushed through the operating-room doorway. The doctor caught Bud's eye and shook his head.

"I'm sorry, Bud," he said. "We got the bullet out. But we lost John. He died on the operating table five minutes ago. There was nothing we could do for him."

Bud Selman swallowed and nodded. "I'll take care of the arrangements."

El Paso
April 8, 1896

Jim Burns walked alongside the hearse that carried John Selman's body. Bud Selman strode at his side, his square chin set and firm.

Burns glanced over his shoulder at the long line of vehicles, horses, and pedestrians. Behind the wagon bearing the coffin walked John's favorite horse, the saddle empty, boots reversed in the stirrups.

"It's a big funeral, Bud," Burns said. "It looks like most of El Paso is here. Your father had a lot of friends."

"Yes, he did," Bud said, "but his best friend can't be here. There was nothing I could do, not even bribes, to get John Junior out of that damn Mexican jail, even for his father's funeral."

"I expect he's here in spirit, Bud," Jim said.

The two men walked in silence along the dusty, rutted road. A half hour later John Henry Selman, age fifty-six, was buried in Concordia Cemetery.

His grave was near the mounds of earth that covered the remains of Bass Outlaw, Martin Morose, and John Wesley Hardin.

Jim Burns and Bud Selman were the last to leave. Burns paused at the gateway to the cemetery.

"He was the last of his kind," Burns said. "The last of the real gunfighters."

EPILOGUE

On April 11, 1896, George Scarborough resigned as a deputy United States Marshal. On June 19, in the 34th District Court of El Paso, he went on trial for the murder of John Selman and was acquitted. Scarborough left El Paso for New Mexico, where he went to work as a range detective. On April 5, 1900, while pursuing a band of bandits in a canyon in eastern Arizona, he was hit by a slug from a thirty-forty rifle. He died the next day—four years to the day after John Selman's death.

John Selman Jr. escaped from the Juarez jail a few days after his father's funeral. The girl he had planned to marry had been sent away. Within weeks he left El Paso.

Bud Selman remained in El Paso for a time, working with the Atchison, Topeka and Santa Fe Railroad.

No one ever found out what happened to Martin Morose's money.

About the Author

Gene Shelton is a lifelong Texas resident, raised on a ranch in the Panhandle. As a youth, he worked as a ranch hand and horse trainer, and rode the amateur rodeo circuit as a bull rider and calf roper.

He is the author of the acclaimed Western novels *Track of the Snake* and *Day of the Scorpion,* and has been an active member of the Western Writers of America, Inc., since 1981.

A newspaperman by trade, he has been a reporter for the *Amarillo Globe-News* and the *Dallas Times Herald.* His most recent assignments were as managing editor of the *Sulphur Springs News-Telegram* and as copy editor for the *Tyler Courier-Times.* He has also written numerous magazine articles for *The Quarter Horse Journal, The Ranchman,* and *Black Belt Magazine.*

He has taught fiction-writing classes at several colleges and universities in the East Texas area.